Anonymous

A Reply to John Stuart Mill on the Subjection of Women

Anonymous

A Reply to John Stuart Mill on the Subjection of Women

ISBN/EAN: 9783337399504

Printed in Europe, USA, Canada, Australia, Japan

Cover: Foto ©Andreas Hilbeck / pixelio.de

More available books at **www.hansebooks.com**

A

REPLY TO JOHN STUART MILL

ON THE

SUBJECTION OF WOMEN.

" Ye whose hearts are fresh and simple,
Who have faith in God and Nature,
Who believe that in all ages
Every human heart is human,
*   *   *   *   *
Listen."

PHILADELPHIA:

J. B. LIPPINCOTT & CO.

1870.

TO THE PUBLIC.

THE following discussion of a most important social problem, while it must fail to set at rest the question it professes to examine, or even touch many of its most interesting phases, may, nevertheless, serve to present it in some new aspects, and open up the field for further investigations.

With this hope, it is respectfully dedicated to all who believe, or are open to the conviction, that their fathers were not all tyrants, nor their mothers all slaves.

THE AUTHOR.

REPLY TO JOHN STUART MILL.

CHAPTER I.

THE questions discussed in the following pages, though they have engaged attention for a number of years,—having arisen chiefly in connection with projected social and political reforms, especially that popularly known as Woman's Rights,—might never have elicited this public expression as to their merits were it not certain that the recently-published essay of Mr. Mill will create a strong public sentiment in favor of the reform therein advocated, while the consequences which must necessarily follow may be but ill considered, or, perhaps, never once thought of.

This is more likely to be the case, since even the name, but particularly the opinions of a reformer, have always a decided popular feeling on their side; more especially when he is supposed to be free from the arts and partisanship which characterize the mere political adventurer and demagogue; but, on the contrary, has risen, at least in reputation, to the dignity of a philosopher, and has been accepted as one of the *savans* of his age. With these advantages in his favor, the changes he may advocate, or the benefits supposed to arise from them, are taken largely upon trust; though their adoption might leave the evils they propose to remedy still in existence, and the good might only seem. Mr. Mill occupies this position before his countrymen. There is, therefore, little danger of his not obtaining a hearing, notwithstanding the rather doleful key in which his case is ushered into court.

Questions of social or political reform, arising among a people whose history has lasted nearly two thousand years, whose conquests in the world of arms must be now nearly ended, and among whom—whatever be the positions of power or place they are yet to attain, diplomacy rather than force must determine results— can never be treated with indifference, or pass without a hearing But this is especially true when their press has long enjoyed almost absolute freedom, and their literature has ages ago received its brightest ornaments; when, too, the most sweeping deductions of ethnology and anthropology are the playthings of their philosophers, and even their religion has been thrown, without restriction, into the hands of criticism. Indeed, a people who have advanced to this stage of civilization are much in the condition of those who "spent their time in nothing else but either to tell or hear some new thing;" and no question can possibly be agitated amongst them, that has any bearing whatever on the present or possible conditions of society, which will not easily gain numerous adherents and strenuous advocates. It is true, "What will this babbler say?" may still be asked by the patriarchal guardians of civil order and public morality. Nevertheless, thousands of those—for they are numerous in every country—who move in the advanced ranks of national progress, and pride themselves in being classed among the moving spirits of their age, will not only listen to any change which seriously contemplates the good of society, but will gladly become champions in the same cause.

Mr. Mill may therefore rest assured that no question of modern times could possibly come before the public that will have more eager listeners, or receive a more thorough discussion, than this same question of Woman's Rights; to which his name has at last lent some dignity. As to the verdict which posterity will give, like all other verdicts, as much will depend on the ability and determination with which the case is managed as upon the justice of the cause.

It is rather a striking coincidence that two such treatises as that of Mr. Mill and Dr. Bushnell should almost at the same moment, in different countries, and discussing the same subject, be given to the public. Strange, too, that speaking the same language, professing the same religion, and belonging to nations equally civilized, and with a knowledge of each other's history, these men should find themselves under the necessity of recording such different convictions relative to this reform. But stranger still, that in go-ahead republican America, one of her ablest writers should take the conservative side and oppose, with great ability, and, it is to be hoped, success, a reform which, at the best, promises only a greater degree of restlessness and political immorality and excitement to a people whose besetting sins carry them already too far in this direction, without any legitimate hope that any improvement or amelioration would take place in the condition of those in whose behalf the reform is proposed; while in aristocratic Old England, the most radical opinions are put forth as the exponents of changes considered necessary to the well-being and good government of society.

It must be that political madness and folly, like other evils, work their own cure: either in the ruin of the nations that fall under their sway, or in leading to the timely discovery of the precipice along which they have been traveling; for in America, where the agitation in connection with this reform is by no means so new as in England, experiments have already been made both in the relaxation of marriage laws, and the granting of female suffrage; but though those changes did not at all approach the sweeping changes advocated by Mr. Mill, yet the result, even of such limited experiments, has caused their promoters to pause ere they should perpetrate upon humanity the effect of some irremediable blunder, and sacrifice the safety or welfare of the state to a mad idea.

In England this reform is comparatively new, and the agitation not yet at fever heat; yet Mr. Mill and his followers, if the case be properly conducted, will have but little difficulty in directing it to that interesting stage, when, like other fevers, it must run its course till public opinion has again attained its normal condition. Happy, when the agitation has ceased, if the nation finds itself clothed and in its right mind, with sense and piety enough left to see the danger from which it has been delivered.

Had Mr. Mill's book appeared somewhat earlier, it would doubtless have received more attention from Dr. Bushnell; as it is, both have discussed the same question from the same points of view, but have arrived at very different conclusions. They have not, however, met; the discussion therefore rests much as if each had told his own story at his own fireside and among his own friends. Arguments advanced under these circumstances at the commencement of a discussion, though put forth with the air, and much of the stride of philosophy, rest frequently on premises wholly as-

sumed, or but very superficially examined. These are
the evident conditions in Mr. Mill's essay. With this
air of philosophy he pursues the even tenor of his way
to the end, failing to see, or disdaining to notice, either
side issues or consequences. He gives, however, to
the public a readable, and, but for the name by which
it is indorsed, a very harmless book. Dr. Bushnell,
on the other hand, displays less of the assumed philosopher than Mill, but more of the rhetorician. Still,
though his arguments, conclusions, and consequences
are somewhat indiscriminately thrown together, and
much of the chapter on the "Coincidence of Scripture" may be but little understood and less appreciated by those not so deeply versed in "angel-sex,"
and "celestial husband and wifehood," as himself, yet
he has produced a more valuable book, and a much
abler discussion of the question than Mr. Mill, simply
because he has noticed a greater number of its leading
phases.

Passing, however, from these generalities to the discussion of the reform itself, but more especially to the
examination of the arguments advanced by Mr. Mill in
its favor, it may be observed, for the benefit of those
who have not had the opportunity of perusing Mr.
Mill's essay, that the main features of this agitation
consist in the advocacy of certain radical changes in
the social condition of women; especially as regards

marriage laws, and all other legal restrictions and disabilities not in accordance with certain hypothetical doctrines of equality to be more fully considered during the progress of this discussion. .

The first fifty-two pages, or more than one-quarter of his essay, is devoted by Mr. Mill to securing a footing, or preparing his readers for the reform, the essential features of which are more fully explained throughout the second and third chapters of his book. These preparatory labors consist chiefly in an unqualified condemnation of old laws, old customs, and old institutions generally, but more especially such as relate to marriage, and the hitherto almost universally recognized distinctions in the occupations and legal position of the sexes. The existence to so late a date of the errors or injustice by which these distinctions are still maintained, and the authority of the laws which regulate them, is ascribed by the essayist to the idolatry of *instinct*, which, in the present century, is said to be greatly in the ascendant.

In order to bring those relics of barbarism into disrepute, and exhibit the enormities and wrongs which have been, and are still perpetrated against one-half of the human race under their sanction, the assumed equality of the sexes, if not the most philosophical, is perhaps the most effective instrument which could be adopted to catch the popular ear. Mr. Mill, however,

cannot be accredited with making any original discovery in seizing upon this oft-exploded doctrine of
equality, though his application of it is certainly original, but withal, the most absurdly unfortunate in which
it has been made to serve the interests of any cause.
Equality as a practical theory, except in the incipient
stages of a reform or revolution, never can have any
weight; for the very first shade of order or government
is fatal to its pretensions.   The equality by which man
may secure power or place to-day, is the very means
by which it may be wrested from him to-morrow.   The
failures and follies of all systems established on this
basis are a sufficient comment on this aspect of the
doctrine.

But if, practically, equality is a myth, naturally it is
much more so.   No kind of mental, moral, or physical
equality exists among men themselves as the basis of
any legislative privileges, much less between men and
women.   The very near approaches which men and
women make to a similar mentality must, after all, be a
very coarse-grained kind of equality, when it is always
measured by bulk; for this is the only criterion employed in making the estimate.   Woman manifests a
certain amount of physical endurance, mental power, or
moral acumen: she is, therefore, the equal or superior
of man upon some one, or all of these considerations,
and must, as a necessary consequence, be launched

upon the sphere of masculine struggles and ambition, to measure herself against him. ⸱ The doctrine, even with all this coarseness, and the other absurdities and inconsistencies which cling to it, might have some force if men were elevated to any enviable positions on the ground of equality. Practically instituted and carried out, such a system would be fatal to all government. Equality recognized, is the god of the mob, and mob-law. The most republican government on the face of the earth dare not practically adopt this theory. Indeed, it is on the recognized inequality of men that position, preferment, and authority are at all admissible in the state, and that there can be any justice in placing one man over another, even with delegated powers.

Mr. Mill does not find it convenient to analyze the doctrines on which the claims for his reform are based; for nothing more nor less than a loud-mouthed, coarse-grained equality, which means nothing, could serve his purpose. If intended to catch the popular but uncultivated ear and intellect, his choice has been most fortunate for success, but fatal to his reputation as a philosopher; for he has been preparing a companion piece to the doggerel, "When Adam delved and Eve span," and he will have his corresponding type of followers.

Every age and nation has its reforms, and reformers

2

who propose to renovate the world, and establish all
human institutions on the basis of equality and justice, and these find hosts ready to respond to their
war-cry. If John Mill flatters himself that the system which he would introduce has a nobler foundation
than others, and rests solely on justice and reason, he
can scarcely congratulate himself on the majority of
his followers and admirers; for these will certainly be
made up, to a very great extent, of those who hold
the most radical opinions with regard to all law and
government; since, whatever be the intention of the
author in his essay, his doctrines are the legitimate
food of those who honor no higher god than their own
crude imaginings.

John Mill may be the most disinterested and law-
abiding man in England, and his design purely philan-
thropic, but his doctrines are such as shall be most
eagerly seized upon by those who only seek a license
to their lusts, and systematically set all law at defiance.
The plausibility of reforms professing to have their
foundation in reason, is never more forcibly insisted
on than when anarchy and confusion would be their
legitimate results. A very slight change in Mr. Mill's
language, without any in his doctrines, would render
him an oracle with those who, like himself, are sus-
pected of great infidelity to the national idol, hitherto
denominated common sense, but now degraded to the

level of blind instinct. With these anything that bears
the form of restraint is unjust and unreasonable, an
unwarrantable interference with their liberty. In this
sense all government becomes a system of tyrannical
laws, all relics of barbarism which these aggrieved
members of society have had no voice in establishing,
and to which they cannot submit. If such things
must be, they themselves must have some hand in
establishing, as well as administering them.

It is among a similar class that Mr. Mill will find
his most faithful disciples and admirers, in his indiscriminate condemnation of marriage laws, on the
ground of an exceedingly unphilosophical theory of
equality, and crude conception of justice. Thousands
of those who are now reaping the fruit of their folly,
in undertaking the duties and responsibilities of marriage,—chiefly from considerations of wealth or position, regardless of the conditions of age, or social
adaptability, as well as those who seek only an unlimited charter for sensual indulgence,—will find Mr.
Mill's teachings the very wisdom of the gods, and
must rank themselves among the most ardent admirers of his system.

But these considerations aside. One of the most
amusing features in these preparatory labors is Mr.
Mill's attempt to convince his countrymen of the justice and reasonableness of this reform on the ground

of their ignorance and utter inability to see its merits.
If, as is argued, this so-called " subjection of women "
has been so long established, and has produced so
strong a feeling in its favor—in the case of all men, at
least, and perhaps in the case of most women—that
it is now impossible to reach their understandings
through their feelings; and, moreover, if this subjection has so changed, dwarfed, or disguised the woman
nature that it is impossible for any man now to say
what that nature is,—pray, how has John Mill arrived
at the knowledge of her equality with man ? and how
does he venture to predicate so much in face of these
insuperable difficulties ? Has he alone risen so far
above and superior to all men of his age, that he is
able to look through and beyond those terrible trammels of universal prejudice and feeling, and wave
aside the mists that hang before other men's vision,
and search, balance, and sift the influences of this re-
motely-established suppression and tyranny of condition or law, and drag forth from amid its heterogeneous
surroundings and hot-house influences the unfettered
woman nature and write upon it, " Equality, Equality
of Rights," and all the long list of capabilities and possibilities which stretch themselves along the æons of
man's future history and hold it up before his countrymen, saying, " Behold ! this is woman !" but telling
them in the same breath that " no man can know her

nature or capabilities"? Surely this, like the impu-
dence of a certain great lawyer, rises so near the
sublime that it may be mistaken for genius!

But how is this thick-skinned, unreasoning, and unreasonable state of society accounted for? Or why is
this particular age so benighted that it cannot see the
beauty or appreciate the claims of this enlightened reform? The solution is easy. "We of the nineteenth
century have substituted for the apotheosis of Reason
that of Instinct." Mr. Mill alone has not bowed down
before the great idol, "the worship of which is infinitely more degrading than that of some former idol."
In his new scheme of social improvement, therefore,
looking from his unclouded stand-point, woman is seen
as he would have her to be, and may again be exalted
as the goddess of this new Reign of Reason.

It is a most unfortunate circumstance that all this
Utopian legislation for the reason side of humanity
will not get rid of human feeling and human instinct,
—that they will somehow come to the surface and ask
for representation in every new phase of government
which may be established to exclude them; and just
as imperatively as this much-lauded, nobler Reason.
Unfortunately for Mr. Mill, names are too often but
poor indicators of what things really are in themselves. Under this eighteenth century supremacy of
Reason, men—the very men who were jealous of

their honor in establishing it—have been known to commit deeds, and be guided by principles which might not very inappropriately grace a reign of feeling, or even instinct; and it may be that under this nineteenth century idolatry of Instinct, men have not lost their reason. The truth is, that mankind display about a proportionate amount of reason and feeling in every age. The topics about which these are exercised may, however, very much differ in character throughout the various periods of human history. But to classify one age or century as under the guidance of Reason or idolatry of Instinct, no matter what philosophy may say to the contrary, argues the most perfect ignorance of even the faintest glimmerings of that true psychological science, of which, it is said, this age knows so little, and upon the study of which Mr. Mill has evidently not yet entered.

The reasonableness or reasonable schemes of any age, like those of an individual, take color from the history of the past, direct experience, the influence of circumstances, and the extent of observation. An age, therefore, does not happen to be unreasonable because its reasons do not run parallel with those of some other age, or individual belonging to it. One of the most reasonable deductions of the present age may be, that human feeling and instinct are not to be disregarded in the administration of human affairs, notwithstanding its prostration before this blind idol. It may be also that ages or individuals, even if they are mad, are not unreasonable. They may only, like the advocates of this reform, be in pursuit of a mad theory, or reason from assumed or one-sided premises. What Mr. Mill's opinion of his own judgment or ability to see and understand the errors and necessities of society may be, must be left to his own self-laudation; but this, nevertheless, is certain, that it is more like the strategy of the mere agitator than true reformer or philosopher to characterize any age as unreasonable, or groping under the influence of blind instinct, because it does not, cannot, or will not look through the glasses which he chooses to color.

It is certainly not very flattering to adopted theories of human progression to learn that this age labors under a form of idolatry which is described as " infinitely more degrading" than one that has preceded it : from which, too, there is no hope of delivery except through a " sound psychology," of which, as yet, little or nothing is known. Would it not be more philosophical in Mr. Mill to put forth this sound system of psychology, and deliver his fellow-men from this terrible thraldom of instinct, before he should attempt to force upon such a benighted age a reform founded exclusively upon Reason ? Might not the age most justly retort, " Mr. Mill, you are a philosopher, and dwell in

so high a region of pure reason; my children are
down so low, groveling in the trammels of instinct,
that they cannot understand your reason, nor appreciate your reform, they can only see your book, and
hear the sound thereof!"

Having thus noticed the very unphilosophical but
extravagant methods by which Mr. Mill endeavors
to create an impression in favor of the reform of
which he has become the advocate, it now only remains, in connection with the preliminary phases of
the discussion, to notice more minutely the premises
from which his conclusions are drawn. Chief among
these stands the assumed equality of the sexes, and
the consequent fitness and absolute right of woman
to enter upon all the occupations and professions
found within the whole catalogue of human pursuits.

Before proceeding to the discussion of these propo-
sitions, it may be well to observe, that no ideas of
superiority or inferiority are attached to any of the
conditions or endowments of either sex, the object
throughout being to discover what position nature
has assigned to man and woman, and how far British
and American legislation has regarded these positions
or relations. These statements are not put forth as
an apology to either sex for any views that may arise
in connection with the further discussion of this subject, but because this doctrine of equality is not so

unpopular as represented by Mr. Mill, and may not be quite so safely opposed as he would have his readers to believe. While therefore believing the doctrine of equality, in the sense in which it is popularly advocated, to be erroneous, and the conclusions drawn from it both illogical and unphilosophical, there is a sense in which it is fully accepted.

What Mr. Mill means by the equality of the sexes could never be gathered from any attempt he has made to define it. It is, however, abundantly evident throughout his essay, and may be concisely stated as the present or possible elevation of woman to the man-type of human nature ; for, recognizing no distinctions made by nature in the spheres of labor, or conditions of the sexes, all his efforts are put forth to prove her fitness for those which man now occupies. But upon this theory of equality it is certain that he might as logically demonstrate man's fitness for all the positions now occupied by woman.

That Mr. Mill feels the absurdity of his position, is evident throughout his whole essay ; for, while backed by this wholesale assumption of equality, there is a constant recourse to a most convenient possible development, and very near approach to man, which is in itself a full acknowledgment of the falsity of the whole doctrine. It is one of the best features in the doctrines of those who hold opinions opposed to Mr. Mill, that not one of them has ever thought of comparing the sexes on the terribly low and coarse-grained basis adopted by those who propose to elevate woman by showing her fitness for all the man-side conditions of life. This consideration alone ought to be sufficient to prove that no reform of modern times has ever come before the public with so little true philosophy on its side, or so little hope of advantage from its adoption; but with so much loud-mouthed blare, and superficiality to recommend it.

It has already been stated that Mr. Mill assumes the premises, and consequently the conclusion from which all the claims in favor of his reform are made. When the equality of the sexes is broadly asserted, or put forward as the ground of any radical reform, he, who from such premises advocates this reform, may justly be required to show how, in all nations whose history has been recorded, in all ages, and under all possible forms of government, woman has universally been found in that condition so pathetically called a state of subjection. That author must be willing to take very much indeed upon trust who, in face of the fact that down from the time when the most primitive patriarchal tent was erected, through all the endless forms of Dukedoms, Chieftainships, and Principalities; through every savage, barbarous and civilized phase of society; up to the most advanced and progressive forms of Monarchical, and Republican Governments, woman has universally been found in the same scale of the social balance. Strange that in no recorded case, nor under any known circumstances, has this order been reversed; but more strange and unaccountable must it appear if, at the beginning, nature gave the sexes an equal start for the same spheres of labor, the same objects and rewards of ambition, and the same social and political privileges, by what fatal perversion of the doctrines of chance, each side has, under all circumstances, exhibited its own peculiar social phenomena! These facts alone ought to have caused any rational man, endowed with only ordinary sagacity, to pause before building the claims of this reform on a vague theory of equality; more especially, so far as fitness for the same occupations and social positions is concerned.

It is true, Mr. Mill makes one admission at the very outset, which is fatal to his whole theory. He accounts for the facts which he cannot wholly ignore by admitting the physical superiority of the male sex. It unfortunately happens that "physical superiority" means something more than just so many pounds of bone and muscle; that nature, when she conferred even this brute advantage, had some work to be accomplished by it, different from that which she intended for a finer organization. It happens, too, that this physical peculiarity has its corresponding mental quality. Muscular superiority does not, in the highest sense, insure superior mental endowments, but it insures accompanying characteristics of power, force, and endurance, and proves a difference mentally as well as physically. If, therefore, "muscular superiority" be a feature which may be safely predicated of the male sex, some corresponding mental quality may as safely be affirmed.

These considerations alone are sufficient to prove dissimilar mental as well as physical qualities in the nature of the sexes, and exhibit the exceedingly loose and unphilosophical sense in which the term equality must be used by the advocates of this reform. But there are others which give additional weight and significance to the views here taken. This superior muscular power, with its attendant mental conditions, is not primarily due to particular occupations or habits of life; neither is the more delicate organization of the female, the result of long-continued suppression and tyranny, but the unmistakable evidence that nature has her unchangeable sex-types, which are not confined to man alone, but are common at least to all the higher tribes of the animal kingdom. Here also the males are in a pre-eminent degree the embodiments of power and force, and display, where they are displayed at all, the qualities of leadership and authority. Can it be that these also, together with man, have from the very dawn of human history been engaged in a diabolical conspiracy to reduce the whole female side of creation to a state of subjection, or the most abject slavery? And will there yet come a time in the transition period—before that happy time arrives when the "lion shall eat straw like the ox"—when this long-suppressed half of creation shall have recovered or asserted its rights, and the timid roe and the silly sheep, with all the ladies of the city, forest, plain, and jungle, rejoicing in their restored liberty, shall display their equality by thrusting forth their hornless heads and fangless jaws to protect their degenerate male attendants, now shorn of their dignity, if not of their mane?

The foregoing considerations, without descending to the minutiæ of individual examples, sufficiently prove that not only has nature, in the physical and mental constitution of the sexes, written difference, but that she has also imposed upon each different duties, degrees of labor, privileges, and spheres of usefulness. It is, therefore, mere mock thunder to assert, as does Mr. Mill, in genuine school-boy bravado, "I deny that any one knows, or can know, the nature of the two sexes as long as they have only been seen in their present relations to one another."

It certainly would have added some interest to Mr. Mill's book had he disclosed the method by which he

has discovered what he thus places in the region of
the unknowable; for it must be presumed that *he* has
a thorough knowledge of the "nature of the sexes"
before he attempts to legislate for them on the ground
of their equality. The absurdity and presumption of
this method of argumentation have already been noticed; its excessive puerility is not its least amusing
feature. It is necessary, however, to show the use
which Mr. Mill finds throughout his essay for this
absurdly egotistic argument.

It will easily be seen that nothing is more necessary
to the successful treatment of this theory than a strong
backing of available possibilities. The very indefinite
and unphilosophical kind of equality assumed ren-
ders it inadequate—indeed, rather oppressive than
otherwise—when any definite claim is made solely
upon this ground. The undiscovered and undiscover-
able world of woman nature is therefore the chaotic
universe of mind from which those most essential possibilities and developments must arise, and on which
very large claims may safely be made, especially before those who accept the popular but ill-founded
opinion of Mr. Mill's great logical ability.

When the right and fitness of woman to all the positions, privileges, and occupations of the male sex are
broadly asserted, a possible development to the man-
type phase of humanity is infinitely more serviceable

than a vague and absurd equality, upon which nature, at the very outset, places her ·unmistakable veto. This man-type equality is, either consciously or unconsciously, the standard to which woman must be raised that she may have equal rights and obtain equal privileges ; and it is only these very flattering sounds that serve to disguise the absurdity of the whole scheme from the most vulgar and commonplace minds, or, perhaps, to render the better, but weaker, loathe to oppose so much plausibility.

Equality, and Equality of rights, are, however, the pet phrases under which it has been possible to clothe in illusory garb more political and literary twaddle than has ever been ranged under any other since it was first trumpeted in the ears of humanity—"Ye shall be as gods !" It is true the temptation is now sounded on a lower key, for it is only said, "Ye shall be as men ;" still, in this case, as in the other, women must know the evil as well as the good. Sad and bitter too, as well as foul and degrading, will be the experiences through which she must pass ere she attain the ambitious heights promised by this reform ; and miserable are the rewards which she shall reap, even from the victories she may win from having thrown away her womanhood and put herself in competition with man, to triumph, perhaps, by the same arts by which many of his successes are achieved.

Having thus examined the unphilosophical **grounds** on which the doctrines in favor of this reform **rest**, and presented some very important considerations which militate against them, the discussion of this phase of the subject might here very properly be concluded. It, however, not unfrequently happens that an author's success, and the success of his cause, depend more upon the very superficiality than weight of his arguments. Indeed, this is most frequently true with him who agitates a popular reform. There are often weightier arguments than he can employ, and sometimes weightier than he dare employ. Whether any of these limitations or considerations influence Mr. Mill in his advocacy of this reform is a question of little moment. A most happy medium between absurdity and philosophy, nevertheless, characterizes his effort in its favor.

Pursued throughout the whole extent of his illdigested essay by the ghost of false premises and equally false logic, there is an absolute necessity, as already shown, to make capital, not only out of possibilities, but also out of the most trivial popular opinion; for it is only when grafted on such popular opinion that such possibilities can have any weight. And yet, if the main doctrine be true, what need of those possible approaches to equality with man, by rapid or infinitesimal strides, to be determined by the experience of the future?

But is there not, after all, this possible equality in the future? And is there no truth in the popular doctrines upon which those possibilities so easily take root—viz., that Christianity and civilization, if not equalizing the sexes, are, at least, equalizing their conditions? No error of opinion has ever established itself on more superficial grounds than this, and with so little claim to a conclusion arising from even the most ordinary observation. For whatever Christianity and civilization have done for either man or woman, they have at least more distinctively fixed the peculiarities of the sexes. It is only when the savage and barbarous conditions of humanity are examined that there is even the semblance of equality or similarity between the sexes. Here alone, if at all, woman is both physically and intellectually man's equal, as well in kind as degree,—manifesting the same force, engaged in the same employments, and often in the same brutality. Here, too, are the distinctive features of sex lost sight of, and the social and intellectual equality for which the advocates of this reform labor, completely realized.

It is most significant that all the examples brought forward to illustrate the capabilities of woman are of such as have put on the man and discarded the woman—such as might make war or dictate terms of peace, wrangle over political problems, or grace a coffee-house club in true literary abandon. If even the Catharines of Russia, Madames de Staël, and Rosa Bonheurs, with all their gifts and graces, are the types of our future womanhood, reformers and maudlin philosophers may well pause before inflicting upon society the consequences of this demoralizing doctrine of equal rights and privileges.

There is yet another, among the hypothetical agents which have hitherto moulded woman's destiny, which cannot be overlooked; for, however its influence may be removed from her future life and history, it is accredited with having greatly modified her past and present condition. It is a favorite theory with the advocates of this reform, and one that takes much prominence in Mr. Mill's essay, that what is called woman's subject condition is the result of cruel, barbarous, and inhuman laws, enacted to keep her in a state of subjection, and even the most unmitigated slavery. If it be really true that woman does occupy a position contrary to, or not in harmony with, her nature, which may, therefore, justly be called a state of subjection, laws once enacted may have almost unlimited coercive power, and might, apparently at least, account for many unfavorable conditions.

It is another of the errors into which the advocates of this reform have universally fallen, to attribute all conditions, whether social or political, especially if they

be unpopular, to cruel and tyrannical laws or enactments.   It is, however, a fallacy to suppose that any
social or political condition is, primarily, the result of
law, whatever law may do to maintain it.   All laws ∠
are, in the strictest sense, but the exponents of conditions, or convictions already existing, which have,
without law, risen to the dignity of law.   Indeed, it is
only when such conditions and convictions are strong
enough, and universal enough, to secure a legal enactment, that actual law is possible.   Even the most arbitrary tyrant requires enough of this element to carry
out his designs, and render even tyranny possible.   In
this way moral acts and convictions had a significance
long before a law was delivered on Mount Sinai ; and
even Magna Charta and trial by jury have also a
higher origin than what is popularly termed a legal
enactment.

Mr. Mill has incidentally noticed this origin of law,
and all credit will be accorded to him for the admission.
Had the historical phenomena connected with this
truth been more carefully examined in their relations
to society, and the result kept more closely in view,
it might have saved him from many of the errors
into which he has fallen, and his readers from many
unguarded tirades against the "legal disabilities of
women," and the "cruelty of marriage laws," "which
still stand, like a vast temple of Jupiter Olympus, on

the site of St. Paul's, surrounded by Christian churches; sole relic of barbarism, coming down from barbarous ages, left uncanceled on the statute book." Are the restrictions of Magna Charta, and the enactment of trial by jury, and a hundred other enactments, disabilities, enfranchisements, and disenfranchisements, relics of barbarism? And ought they to be expunged from the statute book simply because they have come down to us from barbarous ages? The legal disabilities of women and marriage laws may be all and more than they are represented to be, and may have done much towards keeping women in a condition which they certainly have not imposed; but clearly some other ground of condemnation must be found than simply their having descended from barbarous conditions of society; for this, of necessity, does not make them either good or bad.

From the foregoing considerations, it is manifest that the character of any law does not, of necessity, nor infallibly, depend on the age in which it was first enacted nor the conditions of society under which it originated, since there are laws which have come down to us from the remotest ages and the most barbarous social conditions, whose precepts must continue binding so long as society continues to exist. But neither is a law necessarily bad, even when established by force in a barbarous age. Magna Charta, already referred to, is an example in point. What if our much-abused marriage laws belonged to the same class,—were, in truth, more a law of nature than one depending on any accidental condition of society !

This, it must be admitted, is entering upon dangerous ground. For, has it not been discovered and placed upon record, in this same essay of Mr. Mill, that "laws are often called natural, when they are only arbitrary, and the effect of mere usurpation?" But is there not also, if arguments are to be only loose surmises, a possibility of calling things "arbitrary, and the effect of mere usurpation," when they may happen to be natural? The folly of this method of argumentation, by mere supposition or assertion, is apparent not only in connection with Mr. Mill's strictures on marriage law, but throughout every page of his essay. It is an obvious, but very weak form of artifice, which disposes of difficulties by calling things natural or unnatural simply because they may appear to be so, or serve to give a sentence a popular ring. Had Mr. Mill been guided as much by the convictions of his judgment as the necessities of his theory, he might have saved his readers some pages of very innocent logic, in the use of this disreputable strategy by which he disposes of difficulties that otherwise might be found unmanageable, as well as dangerous to his system.

That this is a position felt by Mr. Mill himself is

very apparent from his attempts to escape from it ; for, says he, "some will object that a comparison cannot fairly be made between the government of the male sex and the forms of unjust power that I have adduced in illustration of it, since these are arbitrary and the effects of mere usurpation, while it, on the contrary, is natural. But was there ever a domination that did not appear natural to those who possessed it ?" True indeed, but the appearance neither makes it one thing nor another. The objection therefore stands, and is the one which is so fatal to many of the conclusions arrived at by the essayist. It is certainly careless and unphilosophical enough to brand laws as cruel, tyrannical, or arbitrary because of their antiquity, or the conditions of society under which they originated. But when this false conclusion is applied to strengthen a false comparison, the error is doubled. Are the laws, whether of enactment or feeling, which regulate the marriage relations between the sexes, indeed, so very like those which have regulated all or any system of slavery, that they may be dismissed simultaneously, with the not too imposing rhetorical flourish, that "they have all at some time been considered natural ?"

What a miserably plebeian method of treating this question it must be, to drag up the sentiments or conduct of individual slaves as an illustration, even of the well-defined relations always existing between master and slave, much more so, when it is adduced to illustrate the relations between husband and wife. Has not the language of slavery always been, under whatever form of servitude or whatever master,—whether Greek, Roman, Briton, or American,—"I, too, am a man? True, I am only a Messinian, Barbarian, African, or what you will—but I am a man! You are civilized, wealthy, powerful—*I*, ignorant, poor, degraded; brutalized; *still*, I am a man, and God's justice and the destinies of the future are before *me* and my race.— Three things are possible; one of them is ours: either you annihilate us, we stand apart as your equal, or we compromise and become one." Yes, Saxons, Danes, and Normans, where are you? Where your struggles, and where your nationalities? Alas for poor woman! if her case must be placed in the same category as these, and her condition be really what it is represented, she may delude herself with the flattering doctrine of equality, and take consolation from the conviction of her fitness for Parliament or Congress, the Derby or the Ring; for these are not without their weight in a political campaign. Still, with all these qualifications, her case is nigh hopeless so long as the advocates of her cause urge upon her the justice and propriety of putting herself in competition with man. For, after all, there is left to her only the old cry

which fell upon the ears of now-to-be-discarded chivalry,—" I am a woman!"

Having thus examined, in connection with this
question of natural law, the nature of Mr. Mill's
double fallacy, viz., the comparing of unlike things on
the basis of similarity, and the characterizing of any
law as cruel and arbitrary, because of its arising in a
barbarous age, or under what might be regarded as
unfavorable conditions of society ; the fallacy of the
conclusion becomes manifest which enables him to
place the marriage relation between husband and
wife in the same category with that existing between
master and slave under all forms of slavery and serf-
dom.   And having further shown what those relations
need not be, though arising, or even legalized, in a
barbarous age, in which the law of force, rather than
of reason or justice prevailed, it now only remains to
examine the positive testimony against this doctrine
which thus classifies or characterizes marriage law.
Sufficient positive testimony has already been advanced to show the fallacy of classifying laws as arbitrary or cruel enactments because of their origin ; for
some laws arising in the most barbarous ages have
been shown to be positively good and just.   It is
therefore because more is desirable than merely to
disprove the conclusions of Mr. Mill, even allowing
him all the advantages of the distortion which reasons

from placing a wife on the same footing with her husband as his most abject slave, that any additional considerations are advanced in connection with this phase
of the discussion.

It is not the most satisfactory method of dealing
with a question of importance, nor, indeed, of investi-
gating any truth, to show what things are not, however successful such a course may be in the exposi-
tion of error or the overthrow of fallacious opinion.
Nothing is properly known or sufficiently understood
from its negative side alone. The knowledge of some
positive quality is necessary to form definite opinion
or arrive at a satisfactory conclusion in regard to any
subject of investigation, and not less in settling the
character of the relations existing between the sexes,
than in any other.

Returning, then, once more to those arbitrary restrictions of opinion or actual law which shape the
conditions of society, and, in some way, right or
wrong, limit the activity, or, as it is maintained, the
usefulness of half the human family; is there not,
after all, some very strong positive testimony, rising
to the condition of unequivocal evidence, that these
same laws, restrictions of opinion, and what not, are
natural, and neither "arbitrary" nor "the effect of
mere usurpation?" Are there not, in the requirements and the necessities of social life, well-defined

4

but distinctive features, speaking each its own language, and having an unmistakable connection with this troublesome question ? Have these never-ending and constantly evolving difficulties of state,—these apparently lawless elements of nature and equally lawless elements of human society, which must be encountered, overcome, and directed, to the end that they may brighten the so-called progressive history of the race, —no voice that says to man, " This is thy sphere, this the field of thy triumphs ?" But is there not also another field of labor in connection with human affairs, where the voice of peace prevails, and the language of Faith, Reliance, and Duty is spoken, far away from the din of battle and the clash of arms, and the treachery and intrigue, as well as the "insolence of office," and all those rough hand-to-hand struggles with the outer world, which so often envelop man's higher nature in a crust of selfishness ? and does not this voice most imperatively say to woman, " This is thy sphere ?" But do they not also unmistakably testify that these two distinct sides make up the whole of life's labor, life's triumphs, and life's cares, as certainly as the two sexes make up the whole of humanity ? Yet, must we, like the man who is about to commit a desperate deed, shut our eyes on all this testimony, and dash ourselves in the face of all rational conclusions, to save this brute equality and all its consequent absurdities? Surely the age is not to be so blinded by the sophistry or plausibility of a theory which promises at best only a few very questionable advantages, as not to perceive that it is the recognition of this natural law, and its consequent distinct spheres of action belonging to the sexes, that has dragged, and is still dragging, woman from the coal-pit, from the field, and from the stable, to which this equality would, both logically and practically, again consign her, were it not that the principles of this natural law will assert themselves in defiance of all efforts to violate it.

Examining this positive testimony still more minutely, both the necessities and actual history of human society show this double side of humanity and human pursuits. The necessities are Authority, Leadership, Physical and Mental Power, Determination, and Enterprise; and their equally necessary contraries, Submission, Dependence, Moral Influence, Contentment, and Beneficence; and the actual history of mankind writes the whole male side of the creation, from the gods downwards, over the first or positive side, and woman as unmistakably over the other. Can it be doubted, therefore, that nature has a special place for men and women under the present economy of human existence; and that marriage laws do, to a very great extent, recognize and sustain these natural distinctions so far as they pertain to the sexes?

Among the many errors connected with this reform
is that which recognizes no dignity, no fitness, no justice; no beauty in any position or occupation, if it be
not in some way connected with the physical force or
man side of human nature. For, while it declaims
against the brute force which has reduced woman to
her present condition, its sole end and aim is, to raise
her to this same brute force level, to send her stump-
ing some low constituency, —through brawling crowds
and stinking dram-shops, adorned with all those thou-
sand-and-one demoralizing artifices by which politicians
gain their ends,—to elevate her to this level by sawing bones and cutting rotten carcasses, and putting herself in competiton with man; or, as Bushnell well
says, "by making a man of her,"—the very brute
whose tyranny they have been anathematizing and
deploring.

Is it possible that those who labor for this terribly
beef-and-pudding reform can see no beauty in submission, trust, or obedience? Are they so blind as
even to frustrate the very object of their solicitude—
the bettering woman's condition—by putting her in
competition with man, and arraying against her all
those elements of tyranny, force, and oppression which
are now arrayed on her side, for protection?

It must surely be a matter of some anxiety to those
who have any faith in the progress of the human race,

when changes which are advocated for its improvement, take so little account of qualities which have universally been regarded as the highest and noblest adornments of human nature; when the conditions under which these flourish are branded as "arbitrary and the effects of mere usurpation," because these qualities themselves cannot be made to mingle with or add any charm, or beauty, or power, to the new type of womanhood. Surely, although they cannot be made to count anything in a coarse-grained equality, there is still some weight in moral force as opposed to physical, and some need still in the affairs of men for faith, hope, and forgiveness; womanly tenderness and womanly trust, all of which cluster around what is called her dependent and subject condition, and which alone constitute her true claim to equality, or even superiority to man.

The certainty that these traits are the natural expression of the womanly nature, and that they flourish under the present condition of society in greater perfection than they are at all likely to do under the proposed conditions, shows how gratuitous and ill-considered are Mr. Mill's qualifications of marriage laws, when they are classed among the arbitrary and unnatural, and woman's condition under them, as a state of subjection.

The terms subjection and dependence, while, in a

certain sense, characterizing woman's condition, are so universally connected with ideas of inferiority and debasement that they are wholly out of place in this discussion. They have, however, been so freely used by others that it is now almost impossible to eliminate them. Dependence and Subjection do not, however, imply either inferiority or inequality in the true sense; and it is a mere play upon words to maintain that anything more than a merely superficial exaltation and equality can be produced by the removal of restrictions and limitations which have been shown to be more natural than artificial or arbitrary. It is, therefore, but a weak argument against marriage law to say that woman is held by them in a state of subjection; as, in the first place, this does not mean either inferiority or inequality, if these be necessary to condemn it; and in the second place, a condition of subjection is, in some very important sense, the condition of the whole human family; and lastly, it is the condition into which woman naturally gravitates in the battle and struggles of life.

Having thus examined at some length the claims in favor of regarding marriage law, as at present existing, as natural, and established, in the main, on the well-defined and obvious mental and physical distinctions of the sexes, it only remains to be added in this connection, that in nature's mansion there are no lower rooms; all the conditions she imposes are conditions of honor. If, in the physical world, she has placed difficulties and dangers to be overcome, man in opposing to these the force elements of his nature, in so far, at least, fulfils an important condition of his existence; and woman too, so long as she continues to hold up before the moral world the beauty of submission, forgiveness and beneficence, is also in the line of her highest duty—and shall not go without her reward. But in no other way can either man or woman add dignity to any position than by fulfilling, so far as they are understood, the conditions which nature has imposed.

In dismissing this feature of the discussion, the question naturally arises in reference to the laws which are to supersede those which have just been considered: what are they to be? It is true, we ought perhaps to rest satisfied with the guarantee which is given as to their character; for it is said they are to be founded on reason and justice; they are to recognize the social and political equality of the sexes, extend to woman the franchise, and remove the almost endless list of restrictions and disabilities under which she at present labors. This is so pleasing, and withal so plausible, that it would seem as if there was little left to the unbelieving than simply an unconditional collapse. There are, however, certain considerations of grave importance which have, somehow or other, been overlooked by the advocates of these changes, which must still impress the skeptical with the necessity for caution. First among these is the extremely hap-hazard nature of the agitated reform; for it is manifest to every reader of Mr. Mill's essay that no attempt whatever has been made to show any want of harmony in the conditions which existing laws impose to the nature of the sexes, further than the application of many very opprobrious epithets, while not even the slightest shade of an attempt has been made to analyze the mental constitution of those for whom the changes are to be instituted. Indeed, it is most strenuously maintained that "no man can know what is the nature of the sexes." This, as may be readily seen by a reference to its connection, is the terrible Greek Fire that is to demolish all who hold that existing institutions do not violate the woman nature. But if this be true, how very unsophisticated the admission, since it must be at least equally fatal to the advocates of any new system which proposes to do justice to that unknown nature, without even the advantage of a one-sided experience in its favor! This style of argumentation is so very prevalent throughout the essay under consideration, and at the same time so very original, that it might not inappropriately be regarded as the sequel to "Mill's Logic."

The second objection to the advocated changes arises

from the fact, that all the evils complained of as refer-
able to existing conditions of society, and of which
marriage laws especially are said to be the cause, may,
with greater justice and reason, be traced to other
causes; and the last which need here be noticed is,
that the benefits promised as the result of this reform
are not so manifest as they may appear to its promoters, but are, on the contrary, exceedingly hypothetical. The last two of these objections may be more
profitably discussed in connection with the second
chapter of Mr. Mill's essay, and must, therefore, be
left at present with simply a notice of their existence.

Returning, however, to a more minute consideration
of the first objection, it may be observed, even without
entering into the complications and difficulties which
would necessarily arise from various religious opinions,
differences in social position and education,—as these
would affect the recognition of any legislation which
should place at the disposal of the sexes the same
rights and privileges on an hypothesis of equality,—
that the first and great prerequisite in any legislator
is a knowledge of the nature of those for whose benefit
his legislation is intended. The more essential will
this become if the changes proposed strike at the very
root of existing conditions of society. This is necessary even if those conditions be, as it is argued,

artificial; for an artificial system whose distinctive features have remained essentially the same throughout the whole historic period of human existence, must now approach to something very nearly natural. Whether, therefore, the existing state of things be originally natural or artificial, there is none the less need for this knowledge. But this knowledge does not exist, and, confessedly, is not attainable under present circumstances. It is of very little moment that the changes are said to be reasonable and just. Justice to either sex is that which is in accordance with its nature, and not what is based on a plausible theory. If even that theory should have in it much of abstract justice, it may have so little applicability to the actual conditions of humanity that its introduction might become positively injurious. If the existing bonds of society be so loosened, and the faith of humanity so shaken, in what had long been considered sacred and inviolable, that mankind are set adrift without any gods but expediency or necessity, evils may and will arise of which agitators seldom take any account. The revolution of feeling, modes of thinking and acting, which must follow any legislation which puts the sexes on a perfectly similar legal footing, is certainly worthy of some consideration further than the mere idea of its apparent justice. The agitation in favor of the franchise alone exhibits much of the looseness and superficiality with which the arguments in favor of this reform are almost universally conducted.

For, in the first place, this privilege is claimed for woman on the ground, it must be supposed, of her intellectual equality with man. But this is a basis on which the franchise is not extended to any human being. No man enjoys this privilege because of his intellectual equality with any other man. The conditions on which even this least of legal privileges is extended to citizens of the state have nothing at all to do with equality. It is certainly enjoyed by very many men who, in point of intellectual capacity, are inferior to most women; but they are also inferior to many men, who have as little right to this privilege as women. What about the disabilities under which the great mass of the army and navy, and even the laboring classes, do and have always rested? If intellectual equality is to be the basis, their claim is equally imperative with that of women. But it is also true that thousands of votes are polled annually by men who have much less judgment and intelligence than an equal number who have not this privilege, simply because they have not arrived at a certain age, which is evidently not a standard of intellectual equality, nor, indeed, any other equality, save that of years. What an unheard-of revolution would it at once bring about, if the basis of equality upon which the franchise is claimed for women were set up among men themselves.   Its mildest form would at least inaugurate the wildest follies of Chartism.

No government on earth has ever recognized this as the ground upon which any legal privilege whatever could be granted.   For, as Bushnell well observes, "this right is not absolute in man or woman."   If all government be regarded as an arrangement for mutual benefit and protection, it is only when man is placed in certain relations to government that he becomes responsible or can claim any privileges, and this relation is not that of equality to some other individual.   The only equality which government recognizes as the basis upon which even the franchise can be enjoyed is the equality which arises from similar relations to the state, which have little or nothing to do with intellectual equality, either natural or acquired.

Whether intellectual equality or ability shall ever become the basis upon which the franchise, or, indeed, any legal privilege shall be extended to subjects of the state, what the standard shall be, and how the tests shall be applied; are questions which, perhaps, have not yet even occurred to any government.   For, as already observed, if the primary idea in all government be an arrangement for mutual benefit and protection, till the necessity for these shall cease among mankind, the mutual responsibilities which arise under such arrangements are the only basis upon which allegiance is demanded or legal privileges granted.

It is upon these grounds that the state is justified in making upon man all the exactions that range themselves between military service and the yearly quota of labor on the common roads. When, therefore, woman is thus directly connected with the state, the claims which are made in her behalf shall have more show of justice and reason. It is true, she enjoys all the advantages of government protection through her representative—man. If, however, she insists upon representing herself, she must become personally responsible. Governments, however, have enough of the spirit of chivalry left not to impose upon woman those multifarious duties and exactions which are made upon man, while at the same time they extend to her all his privileges, with the single restriction, that she shall have no official share in the administration. This limitation, from whatever consideration it may have originally arisen, might very reasonably be justified upon the ground that no government is directly responsible to woman, since no exactions are made upon her. Still, state protection and privileges are extended to her, because of the position which nature has assigned to her in relation to her represent-

5

ative and natural protector, man. It must be plain
to the most ordinary capacity, if all men were exactly
on the same footing as all women, or owed the same
responsibility to the state, that no protection whatever
would be possible. Yet all this is persistently overlooked by the advocates of "Women's Rights." It
must be that they have wisdom enough to pass by on
the other side, knowing how fatal such a consideration
must be to the claims of equal rights and privileges,
since these, of necessity, mean equal responsibility,
especially in the face of the doctrine of equality.

There is another explanation which may account for
this oversight. Can it be that men, even of Mr. Mill's
reputed ability, are yet skimming so much on the surface, as not to have recognized the different degrees of
responsibility sustained by men and women to the
state?

That equal privileges from the state mean equal and
direct responsibility, is a proposition which it requires
no very lengthened course of argument to prove; and,
so far as woman is concerned, the whole difficulty is
narrowed down to this—whether woman shall continue to enjoy state protection and privileges through
and because of man, her representative, or whether
she shall enjoy them in her own right and upon her
own responsibility. In the latter case, marriage must
indeed become a kind of partnership, in which each

must become responsible for his or her own acts, civil
as well as criminal. Is it an intentional oversight,
when so much cheap sympathy and drawing-room
gallantry are wasted over the injustice of marriage
laws, that no notice is taken of the very unequal
share of responsibility which man undertakes in the
marriage relation, both in the way of providence and
liability for debt? while woman, if she be the equal
of man, enjoys all the advantages of swaying, directing, or influencing his acts, without any part in his
legal accountability. Surely marriage is not altogether so much a one-sided bargain as it is represented to be, though it recognizes different kinds of
duties and liabilities.

There is yet another aspect from which the justice
of existing laws will become apparent, so far as the
question of franchise is concerned. Though man's
greater responsibility to meet and fulfil all just demands of the state is, perhaps, the true basis upon
which he ought to enjoy any privilege not accorded to
women, yet certain privileges, the franchise especially,
are sometimes granted on a property basis, from, perhaps, the not unreasonable supposition that holders of
property are more interested in the safety and welfare
of the state than those who have no such interests at
stake; and one, therefore, less liable to countenance or
yield to the abuses which always accompany this privi-

lege. But as all property is primarily the result of labor, man may justly be regarded as the maker and holder of property. It matters not how it may change hands by inheritance or purchase, or even the successes or misadventures of trade, all wealth is first set afloat by uncompromising, unqualified manual labor, under conditions which are essentially produced by man. Indeed, this is the substratum on which even all brain-labor is built; for the canvas, the paper, and the marble, through which the creations of genius are rendered immortal, all come through the rough hard hands of toil. Man is therefore essentially the producer of wealth. So long, then, as governments connect property with man's interest in the welfare of the state, he is justly entitled to the privilege which a property qualification secures.

It may be objected, that women have the right to engage in callings and pursuits in which they may, indeed often do, acquire property, and ought therefore to be entitled to the privileges which this qualification brings. Against this view there are two important considerations. First, the fact that the wealth acquired by woman is only possible when built upon this basis of labor and conditions which man has produced. For, be it observed, that all mercantile pursuits in which women most frequently acquire property are but fortunate circumstances arising in connection with this man-labor and wealth already produced, by which both men and women are not only enabled to gain a livelihood, but even to acquire property, though, only by trafficking in wealth which they themselves have not created. The second and most important consideration arises from the admission made by Mr. Mill himself,—of course with the design of showing the extension of the franchise to woman to be a very harmless matter, since "most women would be found of the same political opinions as their husbands." If so, why double the excitement and loss of time for the sake of doubling the votes polled on each side at an election, without in any way affecting the result? These considerations show how very different the bases upon which legal privileges are enjoyed by men from those upon which they are claimed for women, and how superficial or intentionally false the representations under which the popular cries of justice and reason are put forth.

There is still another feature in this Utopian legislation which demands some attention. The disabilities and social restrictions under which women are placed by existing marriage laws have, it is maintained, a very strong foundation in feeling, perhaps even in instinct; while the new, which are to take cognizance of man's necessities as a reasonable and progressive being, rapidly leaving the domain of feeling and instinct behind, are to remove all these unjust and unreasonable limitations.

It has already been seen how very different reasonable schemes may appear to different individuals, influenced, it may be, by different interests, education or prejudices. So much is this the case that it may safely be asserted that there can be no absolute reason or reasonable scheme expected from man without some shade taken from his surroundings. All reasonable schemes or reforms are therefore to be accepted only when, after careful examination, it is seen that they have at least as much to recommend them as those which have already been tried. Much of the success of any social system must depend on its fitness to meet the actual requirements of humanity. But that system of laws or polity which is instituted only because it appears in accordance with certain abstract ideas of justice or reasonable convictions, will be found to come as far short of the actual wants of society as that which takes cognizance of little else in humanity than feeling and instinct.

It must be an extravagant estimate of the effects of existing laws which concludes that they have enabled man to make of woman the monstrosity she is represented to be. If "a hot-house and stove cultivation has been applied to some of her capabilities for the benefit or pleasure of her master, and other shoots have been left outside in the wintry air, and ice purposely heaped round them, and others burned off with fire have wholly disappeared," what are we to expect as the ideal type of woman under the reasonable system, with all her existing faculties equally cultivated, and those which have been frozen and burnt off restored? The best and shortest way of treating this is, simply to accept it for what it really is—a piece of superficial and gratuitous extravagance; nearly as far from a true estimate of woman or her condition—so far as these depend on marriage law—as its author is from comprehending the problem he has undertaken to discuss.

It is certainly a very great loss to Mr. Mill's readers, that, amid all the dark pictures he has given of the evils arising from existing social conditions, he has failed to enliven his dismal gallery by a single ray from his glorious future. This, so far as his readers are concerned, is the region of chaos, from which no light can come, since none has yet entered,—through which the ever-repeating echoes of Equality, Justice, and Reason keep multiplying themselves in endless confusion, till, whatever place they may fill in the harmony of the universe, they have passed beyond all human comprehension. And yet this eternal clangor of Justice, Reason, and Equality, is to be accepted on these bare echoes as the voice and wisdom of the gods; while he who is ringing the changes upon this triangle, tells his readers that the nature of the being, for whom this monotonous serenade is being played, cannot be understood by any man. Surely, indeed, this is the very perfection of unsophisticated innocence, unless the author fortifies himself with the not over-modest assumption that *he* has made a discovery which no man can make.

But not only is this reform *to be founded on Reason, Justice, and Equality,* but, so far as any one can judge, it is intended solely for the *Reason-side* of humanity. For every other phase of human nature is ignored for the future, and condemned in the past, as the cause of all the errors and wrongs which this reform is to rectify. If it could be shown that this diabolical feel-ing or instinct, which has wrought so much misery to man, or at least to woman, and so blackened the pages of her past history, were something extraneous to human nature,—a kind of parasite that has accident-ally fixed itself upon our otherwise perfect humanity,— some hope might exist that, being for a time subjected to this high-pressure Reason system, the evil might wholly disappear. Yet as this same feeling or in-stinct has always been regarded as an essential part of human nature, there is no likelihood that any system of legislation will ever rule it out of court. But even if this were possible, it is still a question in the settlement of a social problem, which is the more reliable side of human nature? It has already been observed that human reason is just as fallible as human feeling; but even if it were not so in its own nature, it is always either the servant or slave of prejudice, ignorance, or some equally potent master,— more especially in any question connected with the social condition of the race,—so that the superiority which might at first sight appear to belong to reason, is very much modified by the conditions under which it is called into action. All legislation, therefore, intended for any speciality in human nature, must always be a one-sided system, based upon certain abstract ideas of justice and human nature, which have no actual existence except in the brain of their author. This kind of legislation, however, is always put forward as the great renovator which is to remove all errors and social deformities from man's future history; while the actual conditions and necessities of humanity are altogether overlooked, or attributed solely to some single cause which stands more directly in the way of the particular reform to be introduced, than any other.

Every one who has paid the slightest attention to the phenomena attendant upon public agitations, will have observed how persistently this feature connects itself with all ephemeral reforms and spasmodic reformers. But Mr. Mill is a philosopher, and mankind expect better things from him. Yet it is only too plain that marriage law is the terrible monster of his imagination, which has placed him under a kind of an intellectual nightmare, so that every effort is directed toward the destruction of the many-headed dragon which has so long been deforming and devouring the fairest of the land. The actual conditions of society, and the causes from which these have arisen, though they afford the only data from which any true reform can be projected, have not once entered into his thoughts. Indeed, he has determinedly shut his eyes on all these, and nothing is positively seen but this dread monster and his theory of equality from the first to the last page of his book. They are the two ivory balls swinging in *vacuo*, free even from the effects of *gravity*, between which action and reaction are equal, so that the first must be removed before the second can become the basis whereon this reform is to be set up,—set up, too, in defiance of the fact that neither in actual life nor, indeed, in any other place except in Mr. Mill's brain, can this vacuum be found. For in the natural world of man they must swing through the atmosphere of human passion and human pride, human skepticism and human faith, human religion, human love, and human hate; and these, as they shed their benign or baneful influence over our humanity, and make the chords and discords of our inner being, are the causes which have made us what we are, and not the best or worst marriage laws that have ever been recognized since the dawn of human history.

The different features in the first chapter of Mr. Mill's essay have now been examined. The views which have been taken of the doctrine of equality, marriage laws, and their adaptation to the physical and mental constitution of the sexes, as well as the question of franchise, and the very different grounds upon which this privilege is claimed by women from those upon which it is enjoyed by men, afford not only very strong reasons against the changes advocated by Mr. Mill, but almost irresistible evidence that his whole essay is one of the most superficial discussions of a social problem of so much interest and importance which has been given to the public for many years.

It is understood to be the business of a special pleader to ignore the existence of any testimony but such as will clear his client or condemn his adversary. But his readers expect more than this of Mr. Mill. They feel, where so much of the air of philosophy and philanthropy pervades the introductory pages, a fair and impartial discussion of the problem proposed ought to follow. Any favorable impressions are, however, soon dissipated by an ill-defined and coarse-grained doctrine of equality, which dwindles, within a few pages of its introduction, to the low rallying cry of a demagogue, intended rather to impress the vulgar than elicit truth. It is not supposed for a moment that Mr. Mill intended his essay should serve any such purpose. He is known to be above the necessity of such a course from position, and ought to be far above it from principle. But, unfortunately, he is not above, not even equal to, the necessities of his problem.

It is too much for even the most superficial of his readers to believe, on bare assertion, that all the evils which afflict society are attributable solely to existing marriage laws, or that they can be removed by the reform which he advocates. They see that the causes for these evils are legion,—that they are interwoven with the interests, education, opinions, and even religion of the people,—that they vary as do the elevations of the social terraces on which the different ranks, castes, and classes plant the standards of their dignity, from the veriest clown to the most august monarch; and further, that on each of these social planes, passion, selfishness, avarice, sensuality, and cruelty hold their revels with more or less frequency, and varying degrees of cunning, coarseness, and brutality. These are the causes of human misery and human wrong which Mr. Mill and his *confrères* seem not once to have seen, but which the world sees, and has seen for nearly six thousand years, and which no legislation has been able entirely to remove. It may have shut up the avenues of escape, and built embankments to stem the tide of some particular evils; but these have always broken out in some new form, manifesting many of their old characteristics in greater or less degree of malignity. Marriage laws are one class of the barriers that have been raised against some of those causes of human misery,—against libertinism and open and shameless sensuality, to protect the innocence and chastity of the family circle, and define the boundaries between virtue and vice.

It is true, they have not been able wholly to turn the tide of evil, nor keep inviolate their sacred trust. But they have·formed a public opinion against these evils, which has done much to suppress them, and confine their open perpetration to such as have set heaven and earth at defiance, and even this is much on the side of virtue. Mankind, therefore, have a right to expect something more from Mr. Mill, in elucidation of his system, than simply the demand for a removal of those barriers, because they stand in the way of some very questionable privileges.

It may perhaps be said, that these evils are neither fewer nor less aggravated now than they would be then, while much more hypocrisy is now put forth to conceal them. This is where much of the safety lies; for while such a public sentiment can be maintained in reference to evil, as that it can only be perpetrated by the hypocrite or known desperado, it is confined to much narrower boundaries. But the objection is not valid, for it is more or less applicable to all law; yet no sane man would advocate the removal of all the restrictions of law because they are frequently violated. This is the great fallacy of Mr. Mill's doctrine.

Many of the social evils of which he complains are in direct defiance of both the letter and spirit of marriage laws; yet these must be removed to remedy them, or should it not rather be said, to grant a public license for their perpetration and render them respectable!

It is not because his countrymen love justice less than Mr. Mill, but humanity more, that the land has been kept even so free as it is from the scandal and evident immorality of the divorce court, and woman, legally at least, free from the intrigues, bribery, equivocation, and lobbying of state affairs.

But much is said of the "real loss which society sustains by this exclusion of woman from the same political privileges as man, since there is always a lack of real talent, but always plenty of unfit persons to choose from." Is it indeed true that there is a real loss from lack of talent, which might be supplied by women, "at least once in a dozen years?" No; there is always sufficient talent for all the requirements of the state. But it is true that it is not always persons of talent that receive the management of state affairs. He who has most capital, most presumption, and least principle gains position and preferment, and keeps them, too; for these are too frequently gained by arts to which the man of honor and ability dare not descend.* In many nations the pugilist and gambler have at least as good a chance for preferment as the philanthropist or philosopher; and it is because this would still be true, if women were to become competitors for the honors and emoluments of office, that these positions, and the contests, and evident degradation by which they are often obtained, have been always considered unfeminine, and have been kept apart from the sphere of woman.

It is of as much importance to mankind that one-half of the human family are kept free from these evils, with their accompanying excitement and con-tamination, as it can be to that half itself that one of their number might now and then, or, as Mr. Mill has

---

* Mr. Mill was thought too clever and too good for the House of Commons, because he ventured to apply the highest standard of morality to questions of public policy.— *Westminster Review*, Oct. 1869.

it, "once in a dozen years," obtain, by very questionable means, a very questionable preferment. If even these positions were likely to be a benefit to the small number that might obtain them, would it really be a benefit to woman to set before her this field of competition and contention, in which she must evidently sustain many defeats and meet with many disappointments, after the loss of much time, money, and labor? It is a matter of doubt whether the excitement alone would not more than counterbalance any good that might otherwise arise from such a reform. The man who devotes his life to politics is scarcely ever free from a morbid and injurious excitement. How much more absorbing would this become in the case of woman! As it is, one of the greatest evils of the present day is the undue mental strain and excitement which women are called upon to endure in meeting even the requirements of the social condition of the age; and this excitement is most baneful in its effects. American writers say that, in the United States, children are born, not by American, but by Irish and German women, and attribute this, which must be regarded as an evil, to the exhausting and unnatural excitement into which the American woman is thrown even from her very girlhood. How much the vital forces of a nation may be exhausted by causes such as these is surely a question of serious importance to the enlightened statesman and philanthropist.

The doctrine that the opening up of this field of competition to woman would better her pecuniary condition, is a most short-sighted piece of special pleading; for, taking Mr. Mill's own estimate of "one in a dozen years," together with the fact that it is only women of education, fortune, and political influence, who should have no need of this pecuniary consideration, that could at all enter this field, and very little remains about this part of the scheme to better the condition of woman in any sense. Those who have most need of pecuniary benefit could not at all avail themselves of it; while nine out of every ten who should be able to enter upon such contests would injure rather than improve their circumstances.

The truth is, that Mr. Mill is so blinded by the doctrine, or mere sound of equality, that he has been unable to see the evils which cling about even the most plausible parts of his own doctrines. But besides this, there is a deep undercurrent in human nature which he has not once reached throughout his whole essay. The cold, mechanical utilitarianism of the age is the moving spirit of his reform, which, as a principle to be respected in the political economy of nations, or in the business contracts or contests of man with man, may be

6*

well enough. But its adoption as the highest principle
which is to regulate the intercourse and relations between man and woman, unless indeed they be mere neu-
trals, acting upon each other like so many inanimate
forces, can only be attributed to a total disregard or misconception of the nature of the sexes. On this phase of
the question there is more true philosophy in two
lines of Milton than all that Mill has written. It is no
poetical figment that gives to the ideal man the attributes of "contemplation and valor," and to the ideal
woman, those of "softness and sweet attractive grace;"
but rather the nearest estimate that has yet been made
by man, of Deity's impress upon his works; and that
condition of society under which these are best pre-
served, is that which violates least the natural constitution of both man and woman. Much might be said
on this head; but it is unwise in this age of positiv-
ism and progress to express either by tongue or pen
anything that in the least degree savors of sentiment,
when the first question that arises in reference to all
that can reach the eyes or ears of humanity is, what
is its use? If it can neither be eaten nor turned into
gold, it is henceforth good for nothing; and yet it is
that in human nature, which so few take account of,
that has moulded, and is still moulding, the higher
destinies of the world. It is not the rough force with

which the man grasps his surroundings and moulds them to his will, but the silent influence that makes the man by the teachings and watchings, and prayers of many years, and sends him forth to his struggles, with a silent longing and trusting face ever before him; to which the honor is due. How much less would man accomplish if that life of hope, and pride, and anxiety, which every true mother lives in her son, were blotted out of existence! And how much worse would that little be accomplished, if every youthful warrior, returning, whether from the field of battle or council of state, with the halo of victory still around him, and his laurels still untouched by any more youthful or daring adventurer, did not hear the old song, "Saul has slain his thousands, but David his tens of thousands," as its notes are prolonged down the flying ages, still adapting themselves, in their endless variations, to the ever-changing drama of existence! But it does not end here. As the evening shadows begin to lengthen, and strange and stronger hands, and younger hearts begin to drive him from the stage like a broken-down war-horse, no longer of any value; while the man-like elements, in their despairing struggle, cry out, "Vanity of vanities, all is vanity;" he hears the far-off echoes of another song, whose music has not reached him since his childhood; and, struggling up through all the cloud-land of his life's history, it bursts upon him with a meaning never realized before: "Come unto me all ye that labor and are heavy laden, and I will give you rest." Woman is the guardian of this sacred song, and as the old warrior or statesman with thin and frosted locks, throws down the sword, or resigns the pen, of many hard-won battles, her most sacred duty must ever be to sweeten his short respite from this weary clangor, and smooth his dying pillow as he returns to the bosom of his God.

CHAPTER II.

BEFORE attempting to follow Mr. Mill through the second chapter of his essay, where his objections to existing marriage laws are more definitely stated, and an estimate of the evils arising from them is more particularly set forth, it will be necessary to glance, at least cursorily, at the spirit of those laws, and the condition of society under them ; or, as it is maintained, the injustice which is done to one portion of the community by the restrictions which they impose. In the first place, then, it may be observed, that these laws are not intended for any particular class of the people, nor any exclusive or exceptional state of society,—that the conditions which are imposed upon the rich are those which are imposed upon the poor ; while the wise and learned enjoy no privileges not accorded to the simple and illiterate. In their main principles they are catholic and tolerant, and take cognizance of all the actual and probable conditions of society ; anticipating and providing for all the phases which can possibly arise under any form of government throughout the whole possible range of human progression.

These qualities they possess, being based on the highest principles in human nature, combined with the natural affinity between the sexes. Besides, their recognition of the religious element makes the principles of love, honor, faithfulness and duty the motive powers which are to enforce obedience to their precepts and requirements. In this particular they are on an equality with purely religious laws, standing apart from, and unconnected with, other national codes; while, at the same time, those who, by the marriage contract, come under their obligations, are just as amenable to civil and criminal law as if the former did not exist. So far also as their claims upon society are concerned, they are on an equality with the most tolerant religious systems. It is a very important distinction between marriage laws and all slave codes, to which they are so often compared by Mr Mill, that, while under these, human beings are born with the chains of slavery about their necks; under marriage laws no compulsory conditions exist; it being a perfectly voluntary act on the part of man or woman, after they are supposed to have arrived at years of discretion, whether they shall or not, place themselves under the obligations which these laws impose. But once having done so, the state, for wise reasons, claims the right to dictate that these obligations shall not be thrown off at pleasure.

Should the state, however, undertake to dictate as to the division or protection of individual property or wealth brought into the married state by the parties to the contract, it should at once depart from this catholic basis; since it is in accordance with the true spirit of these laws to recognize the fact, that when two persons enter into those relations the distinctions of personal property, so far as their individual relations with one another are concerned, ought to be lost sight of.

If it be true that many enter on those relations who, from a jealous regard for their individual property, and suspicions of their partners' honesty of purpose, desire special protective legislation in their behalf, the state is under no obligation to recognize those unnatural and abnormal conditions; since all legislation of this character must be utterly subversive of the highest idea of marriage, more especially as there are many ways in which individual property may be guarded, if such a course be thought necessary. The truth is, that all this protective legislation has hitherto been a most short-sighted and one-sided policy; for it is just as dangerous to morals and to the wife herself, to place in her hands, without any restraint, the control of a large dowry, as it would be to place it in the hands of her husband. If the state must at all interfere in this matter, it can only justly and philosophically do so in the manner suggested by Mr. Ruskin, by which both man and woman shall for a time forego the absolute control of their whole fortunes till they have shown sufficient wisdom and experience, as well as fitness, for the conditions upon which they have entered, to be made absolute guardians of the material interests of their children.

There is, however, one feature in existing marriage laws which has caused legislators, Mr. Mill among the number, much trouble. The state, not without sufficient reason, as seen in the foregoing chapter, recognizing man as the proper representative of the marriage relation, holds him responsible for all debts contracted by either party, as well as all the claims made by government, and, on this account, allows him a presumptive right to direct, to a very great extent, what use shall be made of the united property, leaving each, however, to employ his or her art or influence to secure such an expenditure or investment as may be judged best. That this is the only just course for the state to pursue, while man, as is the case in many countries, is held responsible for the whole debt, must appear evident, especially when it is considered that the contract is, in the first place, purely voluntary; thus, those whose interests are properly one, and, if not, whose life association is likely to make them so, must be better able to make an equitable arrangement than any third party. If, therefore, difficulties arise, or any degree of injustice is done to either party, by this arrangement of respective privileges and responsibilities, it must be owing to extraneous causes, of which due notice will be taken during the course of this discussion.

These preliminary observations may appear strange to those who receive Mr. Mill's unqualified condemnation of marriage laws. The cause of this difference of opinion is, however, easily explained. To Mr. Mill, marriage laws should be nothing more than a series of enactments to regulate a partnership contract, entered into for mere convenience by two individuals, between whom no affinity whatever exists, save that arising from the probability, or perhaps reasonable expectation, that it might be advantageous to the interests of both; but so utterly neutral in its character that it might serve equally well to regulate the partnership life of two men or two women as a man and woman. With this ideal of marriage law before him, it is not strange, though it is very amusing, to hear Mr. Mill, in the opening page of his second chapter, telling his readers that "marriage, being the destination appointed by society for women, one might have supposed that everything would have been done to make this condition as eligible to them as possible." This is not the case, however. But instead, "society, in this

7

particular case, has preferred to obtain its object by foul
rather than fair means, even to the present day;" and
accordingly some kind of Sabine festival must be instituted before there is any hope or possibility of wiling a
maiden into matrimony under the terribly unfavorable
existing circumstances. How notoriously this runs in
the face of historical facts, not only in the present day,
but for past centuries! Is not even the most weighty
item in the scandal and gossip of all classes of society
connected with the arts and strategy of maids for
themselves, and mothers for the maids? all aiming at
securing a settlement in life, in face of these mon-
strously cruel marriage laws; and this not because
other situations are closed against them,—for it is
not most prevalent where such situations are needed,
—but rather where fortunes are carried by these same
maids into the marriage relation.

This extravagance, which is preparatory to the introduction of Mr. Mill's partnership system, is omi-
nous of the manner in which the whole case is conducted. It is no misrepresentation of this system, to
say that it has no higher feature than a mere business
partnership between two men, for this is used by him
as an illustration of what the marriage relation ought
to be. With this view to sustain, which necessarily
rises out of *his* doctrine of equality, it is easy to
understand how marriage laws may appear to him

tyránnical and unjust. But the utter want of harmony between this partnership arrangement and the necessities of the case becomes obvious when it is remembered that the one passion in human nature to which all others are second, is that which unites man and woman in the marriage relation. This is true, whether it takes a coarse animal form, or rises to the highest Platonism. Through every phase it is an all-absorbing passion, and its sexual opposite is a kind of disgust never known among men in any of their relations; while the kind of affinity which realizes the true idea of that oneness which constitutes marriage, has no name among the highest friendships of men.

At the age when these partnerships are formed this passion is at the spring-tide. The man who, according to custom, and perhaps properly, has to do the pleading and praying, is at this season the creature of one idea, unless, indeed, he is the mere register of experiences which have so completely changed his nature that he is no longer a natural man. But this is a creature, or artificial monster, who can sit down and calculate the amount of wealth that the arrangement may bring him, and the number of chances he may have under existing, or greatly relaxed marriage laws. This is, however, a condition of which no marriage laws, founded on the nature of the sexes, should take account, for no laws whatever would be able to meet the difficulty. For, is it not true that the superior art and wisdom of such a monster in the ways of the world would still enable him to wheedle from woman, in the first joys of young wife or motherhood, all her wealth with some plausible pretense of investment for the common good? Not all Mr. Mill's reasoning, philosophy, and legislation combined, were they a thousand-fold more formidable and effective than they are ever likely to be, can do away with the fact, that it is the nature of woman always, but especially at these seasons, to put her trust in man,—to feel the very luxury of love in throwing herself upon his protection, and knowing that strong hands, and a willing and proud heart, are ever ready in her defense and support; and it is not till this part of her nature becomes outraged by the brutal treatment of years that she once thinks of withholding or withdrawing this confidence.

With these incontestable facts before us, and these natural characteristics ever standing in connection with the true and unchanging type of womanhood, it may most reasonably be asked, Will Mr. Mill's removal of marriage laws, or restrictions in any way, remedy existing evils? Upon all reasonable grounds the conclusion would be, that such a change would greatly augment them, as it would allow the evil-disposed, in case of failure in one attempt, to make the experiment *ad libitum.* Every one knows how often this is done even now, in face of bigamy and polygamy laws, and the difficulties of divorce. The giving of a woman's fortune into her own hands is absolutely giving it into the hands of her husband; for if he be a bad man, he knows how, when, and where to choose, and who to choose as his victim.

But there is another difficulty connected with giving a woman's fortune into her own hands, to be withheld from her husband or not, at pleasure, on the ground of equality, or equality of rights,* as it gives to him the choice, if he be so disposed, of insisting, and with some show of justice, that the woman shall bear half the expense of the establishment, the education, food, and clothing of children, and the entertainment of his friends; while it puts into his hands all the advantages of superior force of character and experience of the world, which, as a general rule, will be found on his

---

* The husband is not now, so far as marriage law is concerned, absolute, or even legal master of his fortune any more than the wife, as he is legally bound to spend a portion of it for her personal comfort and requirements. In this view he is simply executive trustee of the united effects. Woman must forego this provision, under the equality and protective system; unless we should choose to establish the absurd system that, when woman has a fortune she holds it to herself, when she has not, man must share with her. It is evident that, if the rule is worked both ways, portionless women—and they are the greatest number—must have, altogether, the worst side of the bargain.

side. On the basis of equality and protective legislation, these conclusions are inevitable.

The fact, however, that these changes, once instituted, must place in man's hands all these advantages, as well as the regulating, to a very great extent,
what kind of an establishment shall be maintained
under this partnership arrangement, for the expense
of which he could not be wholly responsible, while the
woman must of necessity surrender all the freedom
from this kind of care which she now enjoys, would
far outweigh the fancied advantages of the reform, so
far as it concerns woman in a pecuniary point of view.
But this is not all. These changes not only put it in the
power of man to exhaust, in this way, in a few years,
the fortune of a young, trusting, and inexperienced
wife, but they also give him the power, on the most
flimsy pretense, of throwing her upon the world, with
her fortune exhausted, her trust in man violated, and
the whole wealth of her love and hope destroyed. Is
it any consolation, under these circumstances, to be
told that she may try the same game "again and
again?" Is it even any great amelioration of her
condition, that she may claim a division of the children
she may have brought forth, left without the means
of protecting or supporting them? It is surely no
mitigation of her wrongs that she has before her a
scattered household and divided family, but the re-

sponsibility of clothing and feeding a number of helpless children, in face of superadded competition and
struggles with man. And all this because of a stupid
law and unnatural father.

But it is said that the present law puts it in the
power of man "to claim from woman and force upon
her the lowest degradation of a human being,—that of
being made the instrument of an animal function contrary to her inclinations." This is, no doubt, an extreme case, but perhaps true. If so, it is also true,
that many women, perhaps the best, would under any
circumstances submit to much, even to this, before
they could bring themselves to the division of a
family and the wrecking of all a mother's hopes. But
apart from this, would it be any advantage to society,
even to women, that, by the relaxation of marriage
laws, after this degradation had been accomplished in
one case, it might be accomplished, or at least attempted, in a dozen ?

Mr. Mill has, however, ventured upon dangerous
ground; for he knows, or ought to know, that this
degradation is not peculiar to the married state, but
exists in the most aggravated forms where there is
no recognition of marriage laws. How many mon-
sters are able to force this same degradation upon
women over whom the law gives them no control, by
threats of exposure or desertion, long after their true

character has become known to their victims? It is not the husband alone who degrades his partner, seizes and squanders her treasures. The libertine also degrades, ruins, and deserts his favorite, and she submits to it, clinging to the hope of better things,—true to the woman instincts of her nature,—even where there is no law; the only difference being that this degradation and desertion happen much more frequently in the latter than in the former case, often when it is never heard of; since those who have put themselves without the pale of law, cannot claim its protection.

The sympathy which Mr. Mill attempts to create for woman with respect to her children, is another of his pitifully one-sided and short-sighted pieces of special pleading. For, in the first place, if it be right for the state to regard man as their responsible protector and provider, in case of separation, so long as he fulfils these legal requirements, he has a right to direct who shall have intercourse with them, and under what circumstances. When he fails to fulfil these natural duties of a parent, then the children fall under the protection of the state, or such private or public benevolences as can most readily take cognizance of, and provide for their wants, when the mother, or any other may have access to them, subject to such regulations as may be considered necessary under the circumstances; and generally with the additional privilege in favor of the parents, that should one, or both of them be again disposed to undertake the responsibility of providing for them, they have a right at any time to withdraw them from the guardianship of others. But, secondly, as already observed, it could be but a very trifling mitigation of the woman's wrongs that she should succeed in claiming a division of the children; for this, in many cases, could not be accomplished except on the principle suggested by the Jewish king. But apart from this, woman's love and sympathy are not measured by any proportionate fraction of her offspring; for so true is she to the parental nature, that to-day, as two thousand years ago, all her sympathy, love, and longing go forth to the one that is lost, or who is not, till the misery endured over the one she could not see, or could not have, should become the one absorbing passion of her life: just as much over one as over all.

But again, those she might be able to claim as her share of the divided family would, in most cases, only serve to increase her misery, as the extremity at which such divisions and separations should generally take place would frequently, if not always, send her forth to the world as well with a ruined fortune as a broken heart. The responsibility and difficulty of providing for her charge could add but little comfort to the bitterness of her lot.

But further, if the absurdity of this scheme be not already sufficiently manifest, this encumbrance would very much lessen the chances of a second alliance, in behalf of which so many benefits are claimed, and much more the chances of a third; for few, even in the common partnership engagements of life, are willing to assume heavy responsibilities which they have not contracted. But still more, in the "legal separations" which should lead to the necessity or possibility of these new alliances, the errors of woman as well as those of man should come to light. What would be the chances for a desirable or happy alliance left to any woman coming forth from such an ordeal, branded with dishoner? And this would be the case in nine-tenths of such separations. For even where the blame would rest wholly with the husband, he who could be vile enough to dishonor the marriage relation could always show plausible reasons for his conduct. These, right or wrong, would become public property, and could always be used with most injurious effect against the unfortunate woman whose fate it should be to endure the odium and scandal of a "judicial separation."

These are but a few of the evils, and not the worst, that would necessarily follow the changes advocated by Mr. Mill. If, therefore, he insists on taking the abuse of existing marriage laws, and all the evils that may be perpetrated by bad men, in direct opposition to their spirit and intent, and holding them up to the world in condemnation of these laws, he must be content to take the same evils, perpetrated by the same characters, but increased in a tenfold degree, as the legitimate fruit of his easy system of equality, and judicial separations.*

But indeed only a very inadequate idea can be formed of the misery and depravity which would necessarily follow as the legitimate fruit of this system. Mr. Mill purposely avoids the question of divorce ; for he tells his readers that " it is foreign to his purpose to enter upon it." But at the same time he tells them that, " as woman's condition depends much on her obtaining a good master, she should be allowed to try again and again, till she find one,"—that " it is a cruel aggravation of her fate that she is allowed to try this chance only once,"—"that the free choice of servitude (*i.e.* of a master) is the only, though insufficient alleviation." But yet he " is not saying she should be allowed this privilege." What is dear kind Mr. Mill saying ? Has his reasoning from just and reasonable

---

* The late McFarland and Richardson Scandal is an excellent comment on a system of easy judicial separations, as such a system must, inevitably, not only produce endless jealousies after these separations were over, but open an easy way for the designing and sensual to bring them about.

premises led him to these conclusions as the "natural sequel and corollary?" and yet, is he so much afraid of the result of his labors that he must nullify all that he has done, and stultify himself by telling his readers that he does not mean it? At least, just now, "he is not saying woman should be allowed these privileges." Is there not in all this much of the "madman, who scatters fire-brands, arrows, and death, saying, Behold! am not I in sport?"

But there is another side to this question, even in its absurdity. "It often happens," even according to Mr. Mill's showing, "that man gets a bad mistress, as well as woman a bad master." Under present conditions, man, amid all his tyranny in law-making, has bound himself for life, as well as woman; the natural sequel and corollary here also ought to be that he should be allowed to change "again and again, and yet again, till he should find a good one."

If there be anything whatever calculated to save Mr. Mill's system in the slightest degree from the absurdity into which he has thus landed it, it would be, instead of this easy change and unlimited liberty of choice, the protection of a legal divorce in its fullest acceptation. The dignity of a law act, amid the heartbreak and shame of these dissolutions, is all that is left to woman wherewith to face the world. She ought, therefore, to have it in its best form.

But this is not the change Mr. Mill is advocating. He has been oppressively reasonable, and inexpressibly conscientious over the rights of his client, and has given us the "sequel and corollary" to his grand proposition—the equality of the sexes ; but, though it is doubtless the legitimate conclusion to his whole system, let the world have faith—there must be something behind it all which cannot yet be disclosed by the veiled prophet, but which will be duly unfolded when he finds opportunity to look more carefully into his surroundings. At present he is evidently groping his way, having lost the clew by which he hoped to return safely out of the darkness.

Having thus followed Mr. Mill far enough to form some opinion of the prospects which are held out for bettering the material condition of woman by this reform, it may not be unprofitable to inquire what the moral consequences are likely to be. As to the changes by which the reform is to be brought about, Mr. Mill is guarded enough to assure his readers that he is not advocating them. But most certainly, if he shrinks from the "natural sequel and corollary" at which he has arrived, he ought to have dropped his pen till he should have fallen upon some less exceptionable theory for the amelioration of the condition of woman. That a glimpse of the abyss into which he was plunging was the cause of his letting down

8

the brakes at this particular stage in the development
of his system, is only too apparent to the most careless of his readers.

Passing, however, to the moral effects of this reform, it may be observed, in the first place, as a saving
feature, not in the system, but in human nature, that,
even if introduced, it is not probable that many women
worthy the name, at least in the first generation,
would be found to take the extreme measure of sepa-
rating from a husband till all hope of reformation on
his part should have vanished,—till, in ninety-nine
cases out of a hundred, the fortune of both should be
wrecked, and the last degree of wretchedness brought
about by the folly, dissipation, or unfaithfulness of the
degraded cause of all their misery. Even at this extreme juncture the true woman shrinks from the break-
ing up of a household, miserable though it be, and the
scattering of her wretched children, when her teaching and example are the only redeeming influences
calculated to save them from a worse fate,—that of
taking their place among the houseless wanderers of
the street. It would thus be only the most worthless
wives who should take advantage of the relaxation
in marriage laws which Mr. Mill advocates; for, as
already seen, it could be but little satisfaction to the
true woman that she should be able to claim one half
of the children she had borne, leaving the other half in

the control of the monster who should now only accelerate their ruin.

But suppose this not to be the case, but, instead, that woman, with the sanction of this law on her side, should, upon the slightest provocation, difficulty, or fancied wrong,—for there are in the world as many fancied as real evils,—seek, and obtain a legal separation, with a division of the children and effects, all received ideas of home influence and training must be utterly wrong, or the moral results of such a system are too horrible to contemplate. A wretched and dissipated father, bringing with him a number of ignorant, ill-clad, and helpless children, to enter into a new alliance, which, at best, could only be with a character like himself, must certainly be a cause of increasing, to an incalculable extent, human crime and misery.

The evils and unhappiness of such alliances, when they take place under existing circumstances, are too well known to need any comment. Even when the parties concerned may have known nothing of the kind in former relations, the one-sided selfishness, jealousies, and bickerings which take place in these mixed families are notoriously common, and this, too, when the former ties were dissolved by the regular course of nature. What would the conditions be, when these alliances should become ten times more common, but under much more unfavorable circumstances,—

when the scandal of the divorce court, and judicial separation, should become the common property of parents and children? Surely, if alliances of this kind, when they take place in the regular or natural order of human events, are unfavorable to family peace and unity, Mr. Mill may well pause when he finds that his logical conclusions would inflict upon society a greatly increased number of these alliances, but under conditions infinitely less favorable to family happiness or pure morality. All these consequences, however, arise from the fact that Mr. Mill's legislation is founded in a misconception of the nature of the sexes, in addition to a mistaken view of the causes of the evils which he proposes to rectify. This may be most clearly seen in connection with the further consideration of protective legislation.

It is no doubt true that many husbands ruin the fortunes and happiness of their wives, but it is just as true that many sons ruin the fortunes and happiness of their fathers, and this, too, while those fathers have all the protection of law on their side. The natural ties between husband and wife, even according to Mr. Mill's own showing, are much stronger than those between father and son. She will, therefore, suffer as much as a wife,—viz., the wreck of her fortune and happiness,—before resorting to the extremity of law, and consequent exposure of her husband, and division and ruin of her family, as a father will in the case of his son, where the consequences are not so terribly destructive to family happiness. Mr. Mill, in his blind idolatry of mere legal enactments, has shut his eyes upon all this, forgetting that there are forces in human nature that no law can reach, and which must have their course with or without law. It is with these forces on their side that both sons and daughters are able most effectually to ruin the fortunes of their parents, and that husbands, to the end of time, shall also be able, in the face of all law, to seize and ruin the fortunes of young and trusting wives.* Will it

---

* Since the foregoing was written, the comment of a leading public man of Central New York, on the protective legislation of that State, has appeared in the pages of *Hearth and Home.* As far as can be judged, the writer is himself favorable to the movements in this direction, and yet his confession in connection with the operation of this protective legislation, shows how completely it fails to realize the expected good.

" In the year 1848 (says the writer), three years before the Worcester Convention, the Legislature of the State of New York passed an act 'for the more effectual protection of the property of married women,' that swept away most of the objectionable features of the common law that we had inherited from England.

" The first section gave to any woman that might *thereafter* marry, just the same control of all property, real and personal, and of its rents, issues, and profits, as though she had remained a 'single female.'

" The second section said, ' The real and personal property, and the rents, issues, and profits thereof, of any female now married, shall not be subject to the disposal of her husband, but shall be her sole and separate property, as if she were a single female, except as

be anything to their advantage that such legislation as Mr. Mill proposes will give to those husbands, on the most trifling pretense, the power of turning their victims legally into the street, after having stripped them of their last rag? The conditions of misery which should arise under these circumstances would be much more aggravated than could possibly arise under existing laws; since the responsibility for maintenance, under which the husband is placed at present, in case of such treatment of his wife, must be impossible under a system of easy partnership contracts.

What Mr. Mill's precise opinions are with regard to these judicial separations, and what shall be deemed sufficient cause for such a proceeding, how they shall

-----

the same may be liable for the debts of her husband *before* contracted.'

"The third section made it lawful to receive property by gift, etc. from any person other than her husband, and hold it to her own and separate use, 'as if she were a single female.'

"The fourth said, 'All contracts made between persons in contemplation of marriage shall remain in full force after marriage takes place.'"

Of this legislation the writer gives the following result, which ought to have been sufficiently certain before making the experiment:

"It is safe to presume that your female readers are lawyers enough to know that such a statute gives them abundant protection against their rapacious husbands; but the experience of twenty years has shown that it is not adequate to hinder most married women from giving their property to their husbands. Can any female or male lawyer draw up a statute that will?"

be conducted, and what shall be the legal position of
the parties interested after they are over, it is difficult
precisely to learn. The author is very guarded on
these points. It is evident, however, if their importance and frequency bear any relation to the evils they
are to remedy " again and again," conveys but a very
faint idea of the times they may be called into requisition, even in the history of a single individual. But
while Mr. Mill is exceedingly careful as to the minutiæ
of his system, he may justly be held responsible for
his logical conclusions, or, as it is stated, the "natural
sequel and corollary;" for if he advocates anything
whatever, it must be that to which his doctrines naturally lead, and if so, other consequences than those already noticed must follow. It must follow that, apart
from the heart-burnings and scandal, no idea can be
formed of the endless litigation and bickerings, even
on the property question alone, which should attach
themselves to these "judicial separations." It is
well known that friends, during the period of their
intimacy or friendly intercourse, put so much confidence in each other, that many transactions, even in
matters of business, take place between them of which
no definite account has been kept which could be of
any value in a court of law. This would be the case, to
a still greater extent, between husband and wife ; for,
it is to be hoped, that few should enter upon these re-

lations contemplating from the beginning a legal separation.   These difficulties are common enough in
cases of the division of family property, when the
different members have separate interests of which no
definite record can be furnished.   How much more
common and bitter, would these become in the case of
"judicial separations," and the division of property
between husband and wife!

It would have been some satisfaction to Mr. Mill's
readers if, after condemning all existing systems, laws,
and institutions that have any relation to marriage,
he had devoted a single sentence to the development
of his own, further than the recommendation of very
extravagant and ill-considered changes.   There is
surely a very great lack of moral courage about that
reformer who, throughout the tedious length of two
hundred pages, can do nothing more than condemn existing systems, and shrink from his own conclusions.
The vague generalities in connection with the way in
which business partnerships are managed, and the
illustrations of the varying degrees of cruelty manifested by "a Philippe le Bell, Nadir Shah, or Caligula,"
are very much beside the mark, either as a basis of
future relations to be established between the sexes, or
as an illustration of the cruelty possible under those
now existing.   They are not, however, without their
value, as they show the length to which Mr. Mill is

willing to go both in the condemnation of institutions
which he does not understand, and the recommenda-
tions of changes of which he cannot, or will not see
the consequences.

It is of very little moment, that after speaking
with approval of the removal of existing marriage
laws, and the advantages of judicial separations, and
easy partnership relations, he tells us, like a guilty
school-boy, that he does not mean it. The truth is, if
Mr. Mill means anything at all, he means utter libertinism; means that any male and female, by some
easy method,—perhaps the mere registration of their
names and resources,—may form one of those convenient partnerships, and at the end of two years, two
months, or even two days, if any more promising business opportunity or sexual attraction should occur to
either, dissolve by the same easy method. This is no
exaggeration of Mr. Mill's teaching, nor of the effects
of his system. Else what is meant by telling us, "that
it is not thought necessary to regulate other partnerships by law, or that there should be any other condition than those which the partners themselves may
choose to appoint by their articles of agreement?" It
is true that part of this has reference to the equality
of the partners; but it means more than this, as its
teachings are, that the regulation of all the conditions
that may arise should be under the control of the part-

ners themselves. But one of the conditions that may arise at any moment may be a desire of withdrawal on the part of one of the members,—influenced by whatever motive. What does it avail to tell us that "the wife has no such power," when all Mr. Mill's efforts are put forth to show that she ought to have,—"that she ought to be allowed to change again and again till she finds a good master,"—that judicial separation should be granted for the most trifling causes, and that many of the evils of the present system arise because of their not being allowed?

An escape from the terrible round of enormities sanctioned by marriage laws would doubtless be a most desirable consummation of Mr. Mill's efforts in behalf of humanity; but not more so than an escape from the trifling and interminable changes rung upon these laws, from slavery to absolutism, and back again to slavery through all its varying forms.

The terms *slavery* and *servitude* occur so often in Mr. Mill's essay, as qualifications of woman's condition, that her actual state ought not to pass unnoticed. In the first place, then, these terms show a very unfortunate and extravagant choice of language on the part of the essayist; and, if deliberately chosen, mark either a very unfair attempt to make an impression, or an unpardonably slight acquaintance with his subject. For what are the actual and legal facts? In all systems of slavery, the master has the power of dismissing or freeing his slave when he pleases, and of purchasing and keeping as many as his means will allow, or his necessity or pleasure suggest. The husband has no such power. Should he take upon himself the dismissal or desertion of his wife, he becomes responsible for her food and clothing so long as she lives, or at least so long as she chooses to claim these from him. Though she should be the veriest Xantippe, ignorant and useless as a helpmeet, yet, should he dare to form another matrimonial alliance, she may at any moment drag him before the magistrate, and convict him of a crime for which the punishment is by no means trifling. But more than this, if guilty of no misdemeanor recognized by law (and these are the same in the case of man or woman), she may claim a very considerable share of his property, even if she had brought nothing with her into the married state, nor added anything while in it. Indeed, he cannot even legally sell a single farthing's worth of his real estate without her consent and signature. Should he do so, she may recover her rights by regular legal process, after the lapse of years, should she choose to claim the rights to which she is legally entitled. So far does this law of protection go in this direction that even the bare promise of marriage, proved by testimony received in almost no other case, may

render a poor man responsible for the labors of half
a lifetime; and in the case of the rich, for sums measured only, as a general rule, by the exactions that
may be made upon them. This is certainly very like
a cruel and unmitigated system of slavery and oppression. But how are these conditions actually fulfilled
by man? Just as faithfully and honorably as any other
legal requirements; but generally from a higher motive. Is it not notorious in every country, and among
all classes, that every honorable and high-minded
youth who thinks of marriage at all, labors and struggles often for years to provide a home, that he may
take to it a nameless and penniless girl, whom he
would no more wrong than he would his own soul,
while the labors and love of his life are made the sacrifice of his devotion? Where this is not so, it is not
because of marriage laws, but because of their relaxation, and the absence of the principles and duties which
they inculcate. It is true these laws recognize duties,
disappointments, and sacrifices for both; but if the
word servitude is at all admissible, it is legally imposed
upon the husband. What if the law, presuming on
man's greater acquaintance with the world, and his
very unequal share of responsibility, allows him to decide how, where, and in what country they shall live,
and what occupation they shall follow? It only sanc-
tions a natural right, which, if matters come to the

issue of absolute opposition, belongs to man, if only from the foregoing considerations.

But what if, in face of all this, Mr. Mill finds cling-ing to the existing system many evils, culminating in his long list of "aggravated assaults?" Had he ex-amined, he might have found at least an equal number of "aggravated assaults," perpetrated by this same class of individuals, who are found so serviceable in his essay, against those with whom they have no mat-rimonial connection, over whom the law gives them no control,—indeed, with whom they have no legal connection whatever. He might have found that thieving, house-breaking, and murder are perpetrated in face of the gallows and the stocks,—consequences more serious than could attach themselves to any of those "aggravated assaults," even under Mr. Mill's equality system, which system now exists, so far as crime is concerned,—a woman guilty of an "aggra-vated assault," which is by no means a rare occur-rence, being at least as leniently dealt with as a man guilty of the same offense.

It is most surprising that, since Mr. Mill makes no provision, nor, indeed, contemplates any improvement in the moral character of his menagerie of wild beasts, he should be so short-sighted as to hope for improve-ment by simply letting them loose upon society. If the "vilest malefactor now has some woman tied to

him," when her condition is so unfavorable, it could
not surely improve matters to give him a fair chance
of having ten. The man must be incomprehensibly
stupid who, seeing these characters daily perpetrate
crimes ten times more daring than "aggravated assaults," not against their wives only, but more frequently against society generally, hopes to produce
more favorable conditions by the mere sound of
equality and easy "judicial separations." But there
are other considerations which ought to have saved
Mr. Mill from this egregious blunder.

It may be true that "there are vast numbers of
men in any great country who are little higher than
brutes." That "these are able, through the laws of
marriage, to obtain a victim" does not seem so evident ; for, whatever be the defects of marriage laws,
they certainly do not force upon either man or woman
the marriage connection. So far as this is concerned,
all are left at perfect liberty. It is therefore difficult
to see what marriage laws have to do with "their (*i.e.*
the debased) obtaining a victim," though they do prevent them from obtaining an indefinite number. Indeed, marriage laws have nothing at all to do with
this phase of the question, and any less egotistic blun-
derer than Mr. Mill, having found "that numbers of
married people, under the present law (in the higher
classes of England probably a great majority), live in

the spirit of a just law of equality," might have inquired whether or not marriage laws are responsible
for all the evils with which he had accredited them.
But this inquiry ought more especially to have arisen
since he finds it not impossible to realize, under existing laws, something approaching very near to his ideal
of marriage relations, particularly "*among the higher
classes in England.*" Even this is a very silly distinction to be made by a philosopher. Were it not
that it looks exceedingly boyish, it might be called in-
vidious and mean-spirited; for the same facts are
manifest in other countries and among other classes
than "the higher classes of England." Indeed, in
proportion to its number, it is very doubtful if more
tyranny and unfaithfulness may not be predicated of
this class than of any other. Such a distinction,
therefore, can only have arisen from the author's unbounded egotism and self-glorification, or the too trans-
parent laudation of a powerful class in the community.

It has already been noticed that Mr. Mill has mistaken the cause of the evils he proposes to rectify.
When so much good even as he is willing to allow
is possible under the existing system, is it not possible that other causes rather than marriage laws may
have produced the evils complained of? Marriage
laws, as a general rule, have no influence upon the
character till the habits of life are, to a very great ex-

tent, settled, and maturity of some kind attained. It
is worthy of notice that all the misery over which Mr.
Mill expends his eloquence is in no case due to marriage laws, but directly to individual character,—that
under the influence of good men a very great degree
of happiness, unity of feeling and interests, perhaps,
as is possible in the imperfect nature of all human institutions, may be attained; while under the man who
is naturally a tyrant, and given over to all manner of
vicious habits, only misery can arise. Surely, an enlightened reformer ought rather to have inquired into
the causes which render so large a class brutal and
tyrannical than spend his strength advocating the removal of laws which have nothing at all to do with
these evils. If it be true that laws are only intended
for the vicious, it must be that some more enlightened
legislator than Mr. Mill, recognizing that, in any case,
the tyrannical and vicious will rule the weak either by
force or subtlety, imposed upon these by legal enactment that they should provide for, protect, and, if possible, love the woman who might be so unfortunate as
to become connected with them. It is the sole object
of the agitators of this reform to remove these restrictions, which are the only safeguard a woman can have
with such characters. What are her chances for even
the faintest glimpse of happiness, if she should insist
on setting up and carrying out Mr. Mill's doctrine of

equality ?—more especially as there is no attempt made to prevent the "vilest malefactor still having some unfortunate woman tied to him." Indeed, logically, this reform must greatly increase this phase of the evil; for, if woman can risk her life and happiness under what are called the present unfavorable conditions, how greatly augmented the number of such connections must become, when, as it is argued, woman's legal position should be greatly improved, though, unfortunately for her happiness, it is not seen that man's legal responsibility must become much less!

Two legislators on this important question have appeared in England within the last two years. Mr. Ruskin, possessing more than Mr. Mill's literary ability, has rendered himself perhaps at best only amusing to his countrymen. Not because he does not comprehend the evils and their cause, but on account of the novel character of the legislation he proposes as a cure; and yet his scheme, with all its apparent puerilities, is infinitely more philosophical than Mr. Mill's, and would be found more practical and common sense, and very much more effective, simply because he comprehends that the defect is not in existing laws, but in the education and training of those who come under their influence. His efforts, therefore, are directed toward the removal of those educational defects, and the formation of a character adapted to the require-

ments and responsibilities of the married state. Mr.
Mill, on the other hand, legislates either in utter ignorance of the existence of the causes of those evils, or a
perverse determination not to see them.

That the miseries of married life are all, and perhaps
more than either legislator has yet discovered, no one
attempts to deny ; but how much of this is due to the
exclusive character of education, especially in England,
indeed, to the want of all education, except such as
must unavoidably arise from the influence of circumstances, it might be too humiliating to national vanity
to inquire.   It might be too much to tell John Stuart
Mill, that the wealthiest portion of the British Empire
is reputed to have the worst-educated people.   What
matters it that Oxford, Cambridge, Rugby, and Eton
are known to fame, and to the sons of *lords* and *commons*, while the manufacturing thousands of Birming-
ham, Manchester, Sheffield, Leeds, Lancaster, and
Newcastle have no such, indeed, scarcely any educational advantages of which they can avail themselves ;
for whatever little may be within their reach, they are
prevented from enjoying so long as they are ground to
death by tyrannical systems, under which the utmost
efforts are necessary to keep soul and body together?
But it would be cruel to follow this any further, or ask
Mr. Mill how much of the misery of which he complains is due to the drain made upon the life-energies

of all the lower and producing classes to support the expensive establishments of his exemplary higher classes. How much even an oppressive religious system thrives and fattens on the miseries of an ignorant, ill-fed, ill-clad, and overwrought population.

What avails Mr. Mill's specious argument, "that no man in England is debarred by any legal enactment from the highest position in the kingdom, one only excepted, when to the majority the difficulties are insuperable without the aid of a fortunate accident?" Yes, he might have added, the conditions are as fixed as fate. For so long as lordly revenues, that can only be sustained by all but the merest fraction, of the produce of the soil and every other resource must flow into the coffers of the dignitaries of church and state, only the millions of a suppressed population can supply the demand. What matters it that Mr. Mill or some one else may have escaped these conditions *"by a fortunate accident!"* since, while the first conditions remain, the second are an absolute necessity, and millions must endure them, and grow up morally degraded and brutalized under their influence. In this view of the case, it is surely a very slight amelioration of these evils that Mr. Mill may have escaped them "by a fortunate accident," when another less fortunate must take his place ; for while so many pounds are yearly needed to maintain the gambling of the Derby, the extravagance of rising minions of fortune, and the expensive equipage of state religions, only the degraded element already referred to can produce them.

> But this tyranny of existing institutions is not only the cause of much of the poverty and ignorance so prevalent in Britain and many European nations, but it is directly accountable for three-fourths of those evils which Mr. Mill attributes to marriage laws. Here all the tyranny, selfishness, and brutality which disgrace the married state take their rise, both among nobles and people. For, in the first place, those who flourish and fatten on these social conditions must lack many of the virtues necessary to a faithful discharge of its duties and obligations; while the masses, who are degraded by its influence, and rendered fit soil for every evil to flourish on, must carry with them through life much of the brutality which more favorable conditions would have eliminated.

Mr. Ruskin has had judgment and penetration enough to see that these are the true causes of the many social evils which are erroneously attributed to marriage laws,—that the youth who has been educated in habits of extravagance and self-indulgence, with almost unlimited control of wealth, which has cost *him* no labor, and neither the ability nor desire to produce anything of value by his own efforts, must enter the married state under conditions very unfavorable to happiness; while the ignorant and brutal, whom necessity has forced into the factory and the coal-pit, even from their very childhood,—there to receive their education from men and women of the exact type to which they themselves have grown,—can scarcely make marriage laws the scapegoat for the crimes and follies they may commit. Is it not most significant that while Mr. Mill has been looking at, turning and returning marriage laws, as a certain animal turns and looks at a cocoanut, not one syllable has escaped him on these, the evident causes of the evils he would legislate to rectify, or should it not rather be said, to give them wider scope and increase them tenfold? There are certainly ignorant, ill-clad, and houseless children enough in England, and every other country, without greatly increasing their number by judicial separations and easy marriage contracts, to be entered into or canceled like ordinary business partnerships.

Looking at the natural and logical results of such a system, it is most reasonable to conclude that the interests of parents must be greatly diminished in the welfare of children, both in a physical and moral point of view, when they should look forward to judicial separation as the cure for all their disappointments or grievances,—when their loves and cares should, perhaps, very frequently during a lifetime, require to be transferred to new objects, and form new attachments. Is it not in accordance with all received ideas of happiness and prosperity, that the system which contemplates a life union of interests and feelings is more likely to realize the true idea of marriage, the fusion and blending of two natures into one, rather than the system which should render separation and division of children, like the division of pigs and sheep on a partnership grazing-farm, not only probable, but painfully common?

Had the fact, that Mr. Mill finds a higher condition of social happiness — even something approaching very near his ideal of married life—possible under the existing erroneous system, led him to examine somewhat more carefully into the causes of those happy conditions, he would have discovered that it is because the education and moral training of this favored class enable them to live up to the spirit and requirements of *existing laws*, that these results are possible,—that it is because they have entered upon the married state with some slight knowledge of their own follies and shortcomings, and the consequent tendency to make some allowance for these failings in others, that the jealousies, extravagance, and tyranny so productive of domestic misery, are avoided; but, above all, because they have entered upon it with the true religious estimate of the relation, by which marriage is never regarded as a partnership arrangement,

in which there are separate interests, to be selfishly
and jealously guarded, in view of a probable dissolu-
tion of the firm, but rather as a relation in which
there ought to be perfect community of feelings, interests, and desires, fused by the influence of years,
till they become one.

There is still another feature in Mr. Mill's essay,
which, were it not put forth in the very sublimity of
seriousness, might be very amusing, as the ratiocina-
tions of a bewildered philosopher. It is found that
under existing conditions of society, not only is woman
reduced to the most unmitigated slavery, " but she is
frequently able to obtain a degree of command over
the conduct of her husband altogether excessive and
unreasonable ;" " that her influence may be not only
unenlightened, but employed on the morally wrong
side." It must certainly be a strange system which
at one moment reduces woman to the condition of a
slave, and the next gives to her almost unlimited influence for good or evil over her master. If this be
the true result of existing social conditions, it is little
wonder that Mr. Mill has so hopelessly floundered
through his essay, his intellect clogged at every step
with the mud and mire of uncertainty. It is nevertheless true that women are able to acquire this extraordinary power, which, according to Mr. Mill, may
be so injuriously employed. It is also true that men

acquire the same power over women who may be in
every respect their superiors. The error, however,
consists in attributing these social phenomena to marriage laws, or, indeed, to any law known as legal
enactments; for the same phenomena are as frequently
manifested where there is no law, except such as Mr.
Mill has never yet been able to take into his account
of human nature. They are the result of such influences as cause the lordly noble to lay his wealth and
dignity at the feet of the unknown *danseuse*, or the
high-born lady to sacrifice all social distinctions to
share existence with her father's coachman. There
are certainly "more things in heaven and earth, yes,
even in human nature, than are dreamt of in Mr. Mill's
philosophy." It must be true that there is at least one
man in England who does not understand the sexes.

It would doubtless be most humiliating to Mr. Mill
to discover what is nevertheless patent to all his
readers, that he has hitherto been only fingering the
stops on a few specialties and monstrosities in human nature, due altogether to other causes than those
to which he has assigned them; while the faintest
estimate of *man*, his conditions, and the influences
which produced them, have never once entered into
his thoughts.

A number of the leading features in the second
chaper of Mr. Mill's essay have now been examined.

Many of less importance might have been noticed, but, as their discussion would greatly extend the limits within which it is desirable to confine the present volume, they must, in the mean time, be overlooked.

There is, however, among the many errors and oversights of Mr. Mill, one point on which he has not gone astray. He is able to form a correct estimate of what the social features connected with marriage ought to be, and their moral influence on the family. Here, indeed, he is rational, and it would appear that his genius is much better adapted to the writing of homilies than of philosophical essays, for it is only when he attempts to account for social deformities and legislate for their removal that he takes leave of his reason. Had he confined himself to the poetry of the family circle, and the nature of the forces, feelings, and influences which regulate a well-ordered household, he might have added something valuable, as well as readable, to the literature of his country. Had he even made the discovery that, since so many, under the unfavorable conditions which now exist, can be brought so near his standard of perfection, a still greater number might arrive at it, could he remove causes which now grind them down to the depths of ignorance and dissipation. The specious reasoning employed to show that no man is legally bound to those conditions, is much like the theology of a cer-

tain class of religionists, in whose scheme of providence evil is absolutely necessary, and must actually
be accomplished by some man.   What does it matter
if neither Judas Iscariot nor John Mill is actually
pointed out as the individual who is to perform it?
It must surely afford but little consolation to the true
philanthropist to be able to say, "Perhaps it is not I,"
while thousands of his fellow-men, except one, now and
then, "by fortunate accident," are doomed to sing the
"Song of the Shirt," from their cradles to their graves,
in all its endless variations.   Had Mr. Mill taken
up this phase of human wrongs, and its consequent
bearing upon the conditions of married life, he might
have assisted somewhat in making that life what it
ought to be.   But Mr. Mill is not Tom Hood, and it
would almost seem as if he dared not touch this
feature in his social surroundings, lest he might in-
fringe upon the rights, privileges, or prejudices of a
class with whom he seems most anxious to keep on
good terms.

This class, however, learn nothing new when told
that "mere feminine blandishments, though of great
effect in individual instances, have very little effect in
modifying the general tendencies of the situation,"—
"that their power only lasts while the woman is young
and attractive,"—"while her charm is new, and not
dimmed by familiarity."   Is not Mr. Mill really legis-

lating for this class, that they may always have something "new,—not dimmed by familiarity"? If not, there is no meaning in his reform. For all the beauty, unity, and community of married life have, for thousands of years, rested on principles directly opposed to those which he inculcates. Ideas of the absorption of individual interests and the authority of the husband have always been regarded as the proper conditions of happy marriage. But there is surely some other idea possible in connection with authority besides absolute tyranny; yet Mr. Mill seems unable to take cognizance of any other form. The very fact that authority is necessary in human affairs is a refutation of his whole doctrine, so far as this phase of the question is concerned. If one man may, from his social position, exercise authority over another, then why not a man over a woman? and if one, why not any number in the same social relations? Authority in no case can be exercised from ideas of superiority possessed by one human being over another, but from the relative position of the parties. But if authority means tyranny and injustice, then it is all wrong from beginning to end; but if not, this particular form of it may have as much right on its side as any other that exists throughout the whole range of human institutions.

Mr. Mill knows that this is a form of authority recognized by the teaching of all the past, while, at the same time, complete unity and oneness of feeling is recognized, and the most uncompromising opposition manifested toward anything approaching to his easy changes and judicial separations. The attempt to get rid of this teaching and testimony of the past is in perfect keeping with the other portions of Mr. Mill's essay. It may be easy enough to ignore the voice of all profane history by a sneer at barbarous institutions and laws; but when received religious systems give their sanction on the same side of the question, it is necessary to use more respectful language, if it be only from policy.

Admitting "St. Paul's acceptance of social institutions as he found them," there is still, on this supposition, very little sense, and less principle, in his strengthening the evil by the sanctioning of them; either of which must be accepted, if Mr. Mill's interpretation of the apostle's motives be the correct one. Still less must there be in Christ's teaching, that man and woman should become one flesh, as a figurative illustration of the complete unity of the married state; while he recognizes no separations, only for one—exceptional—crime. Paul repeats the same doctrine, only with additional strength, from the more exalted illustration he was able to use after Christ's death. Surely there is but little of the spirit of "recognizing institutions as he found them" in his saying, "The husband is the head of the wife, as Christ is the head of the church."

If Mr. Mill's doctrine be true, there must yet come a time when this barbarism in Christianity—this accepting "Christ as the head of the church"—shall be done away with. These two features in the teaching of St. Paul and his Master realize, with the utmost completeness, the two features in marriage laws against which Mr. Mill manifests the strongest opposition, viz., the unity of the married state, and the relative positions of the husband and wife; and yet we are to accept it all as a mere "recognition of existing institutions." Is it not strange that no approach had been made to Mr. Mill's system during four thousand years, but, instead, that the conditions set forth at the commencement of man's historic existence are the same that are reiterated with a more sublime meaning after the lapse of this long period of change in the destiny of constitutions, dynasties, and empires?

There is, however, no intention to discuss this question on its religious merits. Yet this phase cannot pass wholly unnoticed, as it has been introduced by Mr. Mill, who attempts to get rid of all its difficulties by telling his readers that though St. Paul said, "Wives, obey your husbands," he also said, "Slaves, obey your masters;" and "that it was not St. Paul's business to incite to rebellion against existing laws."

10*

Really, is this all? St. Paul, taking his life in his hand and going forth into the world to introduce a system which should be "mighty in the pulling down of strongholds," is so cowardly at the very outset as to strengthen by his authority this monster evil. Surely the very least that he ought to have done, even accepting Mr. Mill's view of his motives, would be to have maintained silence, and not, by his teaching, pander to existing wrong. But, indeed, Mr. Mill's method of treating this difficulty is mere twaddle. It has not in its weakness even the merit of originality; for it has been used for the last two centuries by every would-be philosopher who has found religious teaching come in contact with his theories. But, worse than all, it is positively dishonest.

It is manifest enough that in dealing with the religious difficulty Mr. Mill should soon get beyond his depth; yet he may safely get credit for knowing that St. Paul has said much more, and used much stronger language, in reference to this question, than he has found it convenient to notice. Whatever weight may be attached to the teachings of the Apostle, the least that could be done by an honorable critic, would be to give him credit for what he does teach, without the attempt at misrepresentation with something approaching to a sneer. The consecutive teaching of St. Paul can only be misunderstood by one who is hopelessly under the influence of his prejudices, or intellectually unfit for the task he has undertaken. When Mr. Mill reads, as he doubtless has read, " Wives, submit yourselves unto your own husbands, as unto the Lord. For the husband is the head of the wife, as Christ is the head of the church: and he is the saviour of the body. Therefore as the church is subject unto Christ, so let the wives be to their own husbands in every-thing. Husbands, love your wives, even as Christ also loved the church, and gave himself for it. So ought men to love their wives as their own flesh. He that loveth his wife loveth himself. For no man ever yet hated his own flesh, but nourisheth and cherisheth it, even as the Lord the church: for we are members of his body, of his flesh, and of his bones. For this cause shall a man leave his father and mother, and shall be joined unto his wife, and they two shall be one flesh" (Eph. v. 22–31),— it is inconceivable how he should risk his reputation on a comment which, to say the least, is either unpardonably stupid or equally un-just. On this passage, however, no comment is needed. It is enough to know that Paul, right or wrong, recog-nizes the relations between Christ and the church as typified by those existing between husband and wife ; while at the same time he recognizes all the love, unity, and oneness that it is possible for Mr. Mill to dream of, chiefly because he seems to have been faithful to his apostolic trust; besides, he seems to have understood human nature, which Mr. Mill does not.

It is known that this kind of argument may have but little weight with the class of reformers to which Mr. Mill belongs. The day is over when philosophers were satisfied to rest their faith on a "Thus saith the Lord." Yet men still expect from both philosophers and reformers the attributes of common honesty; but it may be confidently affirmed that this is totally disregarded by him who purposely introduces the religious phase of this question with two isolated quotations of four words each, to which an offensive moral idea may be attached, and then dismisses them with the miserably vulgar commonplace, that "it was not the business of the propagators of Christianity to make war on existing institutions."

But there is another phase of this religious difficulty to which, as a philanthropist and philosopher, Mr. Mill ought to have given some attention. It is, in many cases, a matter of the utmost indifference to any but himself what the religious opinions of a reformer may be. But it is of very grave importance, how he treats the religion of a people.

No nation is safe with its religion dishonored and falling into disrespect from its precepts being set at naught. Every page of man's past history is eloquent with this truth. So infallible is this rule that it may safely be predicated of that nation that has lost faith in its gods, that it is fast falling into decay. In this respect nations are like individuals, and soon cease to look beyond the earth, giving themselves up to the mad, unprincipled struggle for place and power at the sacrifice of national honor and morality,—joining practically in the brute sentiment of the bacchanal, "Let us eat and drink, for to-morrow we die." All correct readers of history know how much the great and noble deeds of any people are interwoven with their religion, and how soon they sink to a miserable host of office-seekers, setting truth, honor, and justice at defiance, and selling their national greatness for considerations of momentary power, or the perishable emoluments it may bring, when the national religion has become degraded. This is true even when that religion is a false one. Egypt, Greece, and Rome achieved all their glory and their greatness before they had lost faith in their national gods; and with the loss of that faith came disunion, low, selfish, and sensual interests, but, above all, the loss of that high-toned enthusiasm arising from the blending of the religious and patriotic elements, to which all true national greatness is due.

Mr. Mill has not scrupled to drag his national religion into this discussion, and cast dishonor and disrespect upon it, by setting its authority at naught, and making light of its teachings, when he knows that from the first to the last page of Scripture, wherever it bears upon this question, it is directly opposed to his theory. There is certainly enough of this influence at work, without the addition of his miserable mite to augment the evil. As an enlightened reformer, this religion ought to have been sacred in his eyes, if not because it is his own, because it is the religion of his nation, which has for ages blended its precepts with the highest and noblest achievements recorded in her history, and of which she cannot safely be deprived, at least till something higher can be furnished than this despicable reform.

This is an influence which few philosophers or reformers have yet taken into account in their theories of human improvement. But it can no more be ignored by the true reformer than can the products of the soil and mines by the enlightened financier. For it is the secret spring of all moral force and correct principles, which never can depend on the merely contingent and convenient, but on the absolute and unchangeable. Here, however imperfectly understood, the motives to all just actions rest; and no other influence in a nation can be so little spared as that which leads man to look above and beyond the bribes, flattery, and delusions of earthly surroundings, and the passing glitter of a few sunny days, seized by sycophancy or cunning to gratify the longings of avarice or ambition.

It is not too much to say that the advocates of this reform are of that superficial class which ignores all these influences,—that they attempt the removal of no evil by the root, but begin trimming and pruning about the top of the tree, leaving the poison still in the soil, condemning laws, institutions, and religious teaching which have nothing at all to do with the evils they propose to remedy, but are rather the safeguards of society against others of more momentous consequences.

There is still another feature in the second chapter of Mr. Mill's essay which demands some attention. "We have (says the philosopher) had the morality of submission, and the morality of chivalry and generosity; the time is come now for the morality of justice." It would have been some satisfaction to Mr. Mill's readers had he shown how much injustice there is to woman in this morality of "chivalry and generosity," or how much justice there would be in his barren system of equality. Is it of no account to woman that every man worthy the name is always ready to sacrifice his own interests and comforts, and even risk his life, in her behalf,—that an appeal to his sympathy or generosity is seldom made in vain,—that so long as she retains the true attributes of woman, every man, even the stranger whom she has never seen before, is ready to become her servant? It needs no argument to show how much woman owes to this spirit of chivalry in her hours of trial, bereavement, and want, which is never accorded to man in the same circumstances, and which she could never claim on this ground of equality or justice. Is it a small matter that this spirit of deference and consideration is everywhere manifested towards her,—that, as she enters a coach or railway carriage, the man whose locks are gray, carrying his manhood down into the autumn of his days, rises to offer her a seat, and teaches this lesson of chivalry to his sons, which they shall carry to other generations? But this is not all. The poor waif in tattered coat and scanty linen, who has had many ups and downs in life and has fallen into many temptations, still retains this one element of true nobility, often after all others have forsaken him, and discontinues his low jest or ribald song when his instincts tell him that he is in the presence of a true woman.

There is perhaps little danger that any absurd system of legislation can destroy or remove this strange power on the one hand, and deference on the other. But they may become very much degraded. He is, therefore, a most short-sighted and superficial philosopher who disregards them, or would attempt to substitute his barren justice or bald equality for the generosity or chivalry which are nature's justice and equality between the sexes, and which in some form have manifested themselves through every phase of human development, from the generous and high-minded love-pictures of Ossian and Hiawatha, to the purer sentiments which connect themselves with the higher forms of civilization and religion.

It may, perhaps, be said that woman's condition in those savage states of humanity has but little in it that savors of chivalry or any other ameliorating influence — that the heaviest burdens are often laid upon her, and that she is truly the slave of her savage lord. There is, to all this, one very strong, saving feature. When the contingent conditions of savage life, the constant danger from equally savage tribes, and the difficulties and uncertainty of the means of subsistence are remembered, it is something, perhaps an equivalent, that man always takes upon himself, in the midst of constant danger, the responsibility of protection, and the difficult task of providing the means of livelihood. This, like a golden thread, runs through all the phases of savage and barbarous existence, and becomes the power, under more civilized conditions, when human enemies give him leisure, by which man overcomes the difficulties of nature, subdues the field and forest, builds cities and palaces, where woman reigns, at least as much a queen as he a king.

It is true there is another side to this picture. Man is often guilty of deeds which leave his victim in misery, loneliness, and shame, to tread her sad and solitary measure over the "Bridge of Sighs." For this there is no remedy, if the influence of moral and religious training fails to effect a reform. No marriage laws have anything to do with it, and their removal would only increase the evil. The sole end and aim of those who perpetrate such crimes is to avoid the responsibility of all law, for they occur most frequently among those by whom no law is regarded. If, therefore, no reform can be instituted having a wider and more ennobling influence upon human nature than the mere removal or relaxation of marriage laws, the case of humanity is hopeless, and must become worse instead of better by such a change.

The reform which is needed is one under whose influence it shall not be thought a small matter when the nominally noble or wealthy shall dishonor, degrade, and desert the daughter of his poorer neighbor, from the odium and responsibility of which he can escape by the payment of a few pounds, which have cost him nothing, and of which he cannot feel the loss. Mr. Mill is silent on this and its attendant evils, which disgrace every town and city throughout Christendom, and are, indeed, the great social deformities of the present day. All his efforts are put forth, if for any purpose, to render this respectable; for the

most effective method of doing so, is simply to tone
down marriage laws till they shall mean nothing. It
is not, therefore, till this spirit of chivalry which Mr.
Mill condemns, but which has in it, nevertheless, the
true justice to woman, takes such a hold upon society,
that the perpetrator of deeds which now only provoke
a passing smile or vulgar jest, shall be excluded from
society as utterly devoid of true nobility, and shall not
be thought a fit companion for the sons and daughters
of the best members of the community, but, on the
contrary, must find his level among the hopelessly debased. These principles can only supplant the existing
public opinion, when a more rational and less exclusive
system of education is established for both sexes, in
connection with higher moral and religious training,
before which the terrible tyranny of fashion and social
distinctions, based solely upon considerations of family
or wealth, must cease to hold relentless sway over the
actions of society.

CHAPTER III.

IT is difficult to decide as to what Englishmen think of
John Mill as a reformer and philosopher. Whether
he is regarded as the great forerunner of the most extraordinary reform or social revolution ever projected
among mankind,—so extraordinary in its character
that men have not sufficiently recovered from the shock
occasioned by the first appearance of his essay to be
able yet to express an opinion; or whether the whole
affair is regarded as so much beneath the notice of
rational beings as scarcely to merit attention, does not
yet appear, for none have yet honored his efforts with
more than passing courtesy. It is, however, manifest
that no topic of equal importance has ever divided the
political opinions of the race. Not, perhaps, as regards
the immediate results, even should the changes advocated be rendered law; for it is more than probable
that, even under these circumstances, society would
not become so utterly infatuated as to run in the face
of all rational convictions, and throw itself on the
mercy of a mad experiment,—but on account of its extraordinary, not to say unphilosophical doctrines. In
Mr. Mill's attempts to show the reasonableness of

these doctrines, the most prominent feature, except the absurdity, throughout the whole discussion, is the irrepressible egotism of the author. This, on every page, stands forth with that overwhelming self-consciousness which must proclaim itself at the beginning and end of every paragraph. I, even I, am John Mill, ex-member of Parliament for Westminster; the only discoverer of the true theory of government; *the* man of my age and country who sees and understands, better than any other, the true basis of social institutions   John Mill is evidently overcome by the consciousness that some "fortunate accident" has lifted him from obscurity, and henceforth there is no heaven for mankind, especially for womankind, but in connection with "lucrative employments and the discharge of high social functions"   Whether Mr. Mill has succeeded in making himself of any note or importance in the discharge of those "high social functions," it is evident he would mightily enjoy reigning as a god over a house of *commons* selected from among the ladies of England. His self-glorification and excessive rapture, under such circumstances, might, however, prove fatal to his existence; but, indeed, this would be no unfitting termination to the career of the great apostle of this reform. How Mr. Mill, on every page of his book, can bring himself to the utterance of sentiments that carry with them the assumption of superior intel-

ligence, honor, and justice on his part, and ignorance,
dishonor, and injustice on the part of all his countrymen, and, indeed, the whole world, is almost inconceivable in connection with a public man of the present
day, except on the ground of that overweening vanity
and intellectual mediocrity for which he is so anxious
to provide by this reform. But, indeed, this is no
hypothetical conclusion; for no work making any pre-
tentions to philosophy has been given to the public for
three centuries that has so little to recommend it, except the mere dictum of its author. On the first page
of the third chapter occurs the following: " I believe
that their disabilities, elsewhere, are only clung to in
order to maintain their subordination in domestic life;
because the generality of the male sex cannot yet tolerate the idea of living with an equal." Here comes
the evidence that Mr. Mill is still in his boyhood, so
manifestly a novice, and so terribly oppressed with the
consciousness that he, during a few months in the year,
has been, if not making laws, at least where laws are
made, and therefore fancies that all men, like himself,
live constantly with the consciousness of legal enactments hanging over their heads, like the sword of
Dionysius. Had he even common discernment, he
would have discovered that thousands of men not only
tolerate the idea, but the fact, and live during a long
married life not only with equals but superiors, without

once entertaining the thought that they possess any legal superiority. But what does Mr. Mill mean by an equal? It is evident that a mere legal enactment will not make those equal, in any important sense, who are not so already. But if it be simply legal equality that is meant, then every business partnership, which not only exists between men, but frequently between men and women, is an evidence disproving Mr. Mill's doctrine; and even if such did not exist, it certainly would tax his ingenuity to show why man might not tolerate legal equality as well with women as with men. This, however, has little to do with the main doctrines advanced in the third chapter, further than showing the absurdities into which the author plunges at the very outset.

The doctrine of equality, which plays so important a part in the opening chapter, is again brought into requisition in the third, chiefly to show woman's fitness for all those official positions and occupations now supposed proper to men. If the efforts which an advocate puts forth are generally in proportion to the hopelessness and conscious weakness of his cause, then no man in England is so much impressed with the inequality of the sexes as Mr. Mill. Indeed, it is more than probable that not a hundred men in the British Islands, whose opinion is worth any consideration, believe the sexes unequal in any high sense; nor had such an idea ever entered the public mind till this latest philosopher, who seems to have been sleeping for the last thirty years in the cave of self-sufficiency, comes forth to remodel the nation and enlighten the world. It is to be hoped that Englishmen do now look upon women as the equals of men, and have no need of this second Mohammed's coming forth to impose upon the race his coarse-grained theories of equality, and build up another paradise, which woman can only enter by the discharge of "high social functions." Well, Mr. Mill has arrived at this enviable station, and has been made legally equal to every other man in the same sphere. Is it not a monstrous injustice that he cannot there find high social functions to be discharged by every woman in the kingdom, and make them all at least legally equal to himself?

That Mr. Mill is legislating for a particular class has already been observed; if otherwise, he is the most short-sighted and imbecile reformer that has ever attempted to benefit mankind. What are his lucrative situations and high social functions to do for the thousands of poverty-stricken and ignorant women throughout the nation, when, for every vacancy that now occurs, there are an unlimited number of candidates? Is it not now too true, that "offices, lucrative positions, and high social functions" must be found for men, rather than men for these? It would, no doubt, be comfortable enough if Mrs. A, Mrs. B, or Mrs. M, could control the exchequer, become Lady Privy Seal, or Secretary of War; but if these are the only results, as they are the only advantages that take prominence in this agitation, what about high-minded philanthropy, the peculiar characteristic arrogated by Mr. Mill?

The grounds upon which these seeming advantages are claimed for woman have already been noticed in the first part of this discussion. It is unnecessary, therefore, to do anything more now than repeat the facts, showing these claims to be made for women on very different grounds from those upon which they are granted to men. Mr. Mill must therefore do something more for woman than prove her equality with man before she can justly enjoy his legal privileges, even if this were an improvement of her condition, which does not appear from the labors of her advocate. He must, to secure these privileges, render her liable to military service, to take her place before the mast, to perform the public labors imposed by governments in many countries, and she must also become responsible for a proportionate share of the public revenue, as well as all debts contracted by her under any circumstances wherein man would now become liable, with all the changes which must inevitably take place in her domestic relations, in the way of additional responsibility for a proportionate share of family expense. This is the kind of equality which Mr Mill must bring about before his client can justly enjoy the legal privileges which he claims for her, and not an intellectual equality, which perhaps no sensible man in England doubts, except Mr. Mill himself,—at least no other considers so many real and possible changes necessary before this equality can be attained.

But as Mr. Mill is perhaps the only man in England who doubts the equality of the sexes on any elevated basis, he is, perhaps, also the only one who holds that equal legal privileges ought to be enjoyed solely on this ground at the expense of every other consideration. There are many public men in England, having intellectual ability sufficient to set up in business a number of men of Mr. Mill's caliber, who have never yet doubted the equality of their wives with themselves, but who would shrink, as from utter pollution, from throwing those wives into the arena of political life and the struggles for power and place which always accompany it. So blind is Mr. Mill to this feature of the question, that throughout the whole of his essay he appears like an overgrown boy who had been reared by his grandmother, in the perfect innocence of a young Lavinia, doubtless, but with the conceit and self-sufficiency which arises from the mutual glorification of two such natures—producing the pleasing conviction that there are in the world only two such beings, the wonderful boy and his wonderful grand mother. In this particular instance, there is the additional amusing circumstance that the boy, and perhaps his grandmother, entertains the further conviction that he is to revolutionize the world.

But apart from the conscious attempts at complaisance and half conceited, half good-natured reasonableness which have evidently grown out of the inability to support with equanimity the dignity of his position, Mr. Mill is much like the Cockney who had never learned there was a world outside of London; for, if he were not utterly blind to the real evils and necessities of society, he could not bring himself to the constant reiteration of the injustice of excluding woman from a chance "for high social distinctions." Perhaps Mr. Mill does not know that every true woman feels herself equally honored in the honor of her husband. If distinction, therefore, be all, she cannot increase this. The other advantages, as already seen, are exceedingly doubtful. If the good of woman be actually the question at issue, why can nothing be done for those who really require a reformation in their morals as well as material conditions? This reform will never reach the thousands whose lives are doomed to poverty, hunger, dirt, and ignorance. What are lucrative positions or the franchise

to these, when there are now thousands of educated
men who cannot obtain "enviable positions and distinctions," often better fitted for them than those who
do? But what would they do, even for the women
who do obtain them under Mr. Mill's *régime?* What
do they now do for the men who obtain them? Is it
not true that every *honorable* public man increases
his poverty rather than his wealth by devotion to the
service of his country? How much more would this
be the case when the competition should be doubled?
But, again, out of six or eight of the higher professions, only three are closed against woman, and these
the most limited; for in Politics, the Church, and
Law, only a very limited number of changes occur
during a lifetime. On the other hand, the whole field
of the fine arts,—Painting, Poetry, Sculpture, and
Music, with Science, Philosophy, and a very important
department in Medicine, has long been open to free
competition between the sexes. The character of the
competition in these is also very different from what it
is in the former. In politics and law, especially, very
often only rough, brazen-faced opposition, if not im-
pudence, are the requisites to success, not to speak
of bribery and the dishonorable strategy by which
ends are accomplished. This alone, if there were no
others, would afford sufficient reason for excluding
woman from a competition which has not a single re-

deeming feature in its favor,—more especially as any one of the other fields to which women are admitted is wider than law and politics put together, so far as the mere situations in connection with them are concerned, and no woman is prohibited from entering the field with Coke or Blackstone, Smith or Ricardo. If, therefore, these "lucrative situations and high social positions" are not to be a mere sinecure, thrown to woman without the troubles and responsibilities which accompany them,—a course both unjust and unphilosophical, as well as immoral in its tendencies,—the advantages are more than counterbalanced by the responsibilities alone, which would necessarily be increased tenfold. At present, woman is legally free from the cares, duties, and disappointments connected with the administration of state affairs. Will the mere contingent advantages claimed by Mr. Mill be found an equivalent for the loss of this freedom? If not something more than an equivalent, no good, even pecuniarily, can arise from the change. But there is another consideration which, according to Mr. Mill, ought to induce mankind to embrace this reform. Much loss arises to the country from the non-employment of so much available talent. The day is over when this argument could have much weight. It has already been seen that real worth and talent have often the poorest chance of success. But, beside this, the artificial system under which it was possible for public men to bring into the council-chambers of the nation weapons of death, merely for rhetorical effect, is passing away. As civilization, in its progress, equalizes mankind, these phases in the social phenomena of nations are toned down to the quiet level of common sense. This, more than inflammatory oratorical appeals or labored perorations, is the great desideratum in the government of empires. It would doubtless be a moment of high inspiration if, in the hour of great national danger, the most beautiful and talented woman in the realm should, with bosom bare, toga floating in the wind, and drawn dagger pointed at her breast, come forth, uttering, with more than the enthusiasm of a Patrick Henry, "As for me, give me liberty, or give me death!" But men do not legislate for these situations. When they do occur, there is always a Joan of Arc to save the nation,—her power doubled, from the fact that she has never been the tool or slave of political factions, which woman would evidently become should Mr. Mill ever succeed in imposing his reform upon mankind. The cry, therefore, as to loss sustained from unemployed talent, which is put forth in the first chapter of Mr. Mill's essay, and again repeated in the third, can only arise from the manifest importance attached to abilities of the same order as his own, or the utter inability to comprehend the real necessities of society,—a condition of mind arising from the oppressive egotism which attempts to impose upon his readers, on every page of his book, the belief, which he has evidently imposed upon himself, that there is nothing in heaven or earth so important to the world of man, as that Mr. Mill should be employed in the discharge of high social functions. But there is another plea put forth, which may have weight with certain classes. It is maintained to be injustice to woman that she should be excluded from, at least, the liberty of trying the good or evil of public life, and thus testing by personal experience her fitness to engage in its contests and sustain its reverses. It may be said that little harm could arise from permitting the experiment. But, in order to make even the experiment, the very foundations of all existing social institutions must be destroyed, and a power for evil unchained, which cannot again be brought under control. With men of Mr. Mill's style of gallantry and peculiar mentality, the mere reiteration of the words justice, liberty, or equality, have a peculiar effect. The sounds alone take the place of reason or argument, and they become blind and dumb in presence of their own philosophical paradoxes. Any claim, therefore, made for woman on the ground of reason or justice, cannot be safely opposed with this class, whose highest phi-

losophy consists in mere assertion, and who become
so enamored of their own schemes and fancies that
no counter-influence is even so much as noticed. The
case in hand is an excellent illustration of this fact.
Mr. Mill, from beginning to end of the third chapter
of his essay, has rested all the claims of his reform
on nothing higher than his choosing to say it would
be an advantage to woman, and therefore justice.
The advantages he has not attempted to show; the
loss is perhaps patent to all but himself; for, in all
questions affecting the conditions of society, justice
to man or woman does not consist in any course of
action based upon mere abstract ideas of liberty or
equality, but in what, after taking all the circumstances into account, may appear to be the greatest
good to mankind. But apart from this general truth,
justice to woman does not consist in merely asserting
that the two sides of humanity, independent of sexual
distinctions, are equally fitted for all the occupations,
professions, and responsibilities which range themselves from the highest to the lowest of human institutions. If such a proposition be true, something
more than mere assertion is necessary to prove what
runs counter to all received ideas of propriety, or
even of justice. It may be all very well, and doubtless very conclusive, to attribute these ideas of justice
and propriety to the idolatry of instinct, or some

equally obscure agent, in the absence of any other argument, but it is still within the bounds of probability that the great mass of mankind may, in this instance, be right, and Mr. Mill wrong; that the agitations which may yet arise in connection with this question will only serve to prove more clearly that what is justice to man is not justice to woman, and what is justice to woman is not justice to man; that, in connection with the functions of government, to woman belongs the potential though silent influence which may be exerted by her advice, example, or force of character,—to man the responsibility, administrative and official duty. If more or less than this is justice to either sex, then Mr. Mill has failed most signally to show how or why, unless, indeed, his mere dictum be received by his readers in preference to their own reasonable convictions.

There is, however, another difficulty connected with this discharge of high social functions, viz., the remodeling of the whole system of female education. It is true that this, even apart from these considerations, is one of the social reforms most urgently needed in the present day. But that it should take the shape of preparing women for high social functions which one in a hundred thousand would not be called upon to fulfil, is certainly neither very philosophical nor practical. Besides, it is a perversion of

12*

all our ideas of the character and sphere of woman
to suppose it necessary, in fitting her for the duties of
life, that the weight of her education should arise
from contact with that order of mentality of which
Coke, Blackstone, Adam Smith, Bacon, Locke, and
Kant are the types. It is true, male legislators are
not always oppressed with lore drawn from these
sources. But it is, nevertheless, true that the kind of
mentality of which these furnish an example is the
great prerequisite in any high order of statesmanship.
Of lower orders there is, according to Mr. Mill, a sufficient supply. If, therefore, he is compelled to admit
that "no production in philosophy, science, or art, entitled to the first rank, has been the production of
woman," what is the balance in favor of this reform,
even on the ground of utility? and how radical the
revolution necessary before woman shall to any extent
acquire a fitness for those high functions and duties
which are maintained to be within her legitimate
sphere? The fact that Mr. Mill has been able to furnish a few examples of women who have manifested
high capabilities as rulers, is no more to the point than
if he should maintain the fitness of men for all the
occupations now thought to belong to women, because
some men have manifested a passion for embroidery.
But apart from this, examples chosen from the
spheres which Mr. Mill has found most serviceable to

his theory, are very exceptional, both as to number and circumstances. Rulers of any limited monarchy are little more than the great seal which gives authority to state documents. The goodness or badness of a monarch under such a constitution as that of England depends chiefly on the character of the crown advisers. It very often happens under these circumstances, that the man or woman who has least individuality is the best ruler, as the character of any reign depends more on the united wisdom of the responsible ministers of the crown than the individual character of the sovereign. In accordance with this view, better government may be expected under a woman than under a man, simply because it is her nature to submit to influences and authority; while man would be found more frequently opposing his individual wisdom to the united wisdom of the nation. The position of the sovereign, however, is an exceptional case, and affords no argument in favor of Mr. Mill's general doctrine, but rather another instance of false logic, by which a general principle is deduced from an extremely limited premiss. Indeed, the whole testimony of English and European history, wherever woman has connected herself with government as an adviser, or mingled in the intrigues and diplomacy of courts, is unfavorable to Mr. Mill's theory. Whatever may be said of woman in discharging the duties of royalty, a careful examination of facts will show that they are due more to the simple quality of submission than to any higher demonstrative characteristics. Queen Elizabeth, who is often brought forward as an example of woman's ability to govern, owes her best achievements to this single quality. Had she been possessed of the obstinacy of her father, not all her intellectual qualities would have saved her from infamy.* Is it not also notorious that no other reign in English history, either before or after, displays such a galaxy of philosophical, administrative, and literary ability? How much of Elizabeth's success is due even to the public opinion formed by the men of her time is quite pertinent to the question in hand. The very reaction from the atrocities of the former reign is much in her favor. It may, therefore, safely be concluded that the character of this reign does not depend so much on Elizabeth as upon her advisers, and the circumstances under which she ascended the throne. It is admitted that just as much may be said of the reign of any man, with this slight exception, that the effects either for good or evil will be due in a greater degree to the man's personal character. Examples, therefore, taken from among men or women who are born to positions, have very

---

* Those who are enamored of the ability of Queen Elizabeth as a ruler, or her character as a woman, are referred to the latest estimate of these by Froude.

little weight in this discussion. Even under an absolute monarchy the force of established custom trammels and restrains the natural disposition to such an
extent that it is only when a number of sovereigns of
very decided individuality succeed each other, that any
important change can be effected in established forms
and institutions. If it could be shown that as many,
or any respectable number of women, among any people, or in any nation, had struggled up side by side
with men to the same positions, duties, and occupations, then the argument would have some weight.
It will not serve to say that cruel laws and physical
force have produced the result. Cruel laws and physical force have been employed to keep classes of men
in subjection, but *these* have ruled the makers of the
laws, and turned the forces against them. It cannot,
however, be shown that any united effort has ever
been made to reduce woman to the condition in which
she is found. The strongest conspiracy ever instituted
against her was that headed by Romulus, who con-
templated no permanent institution to be perpetuated
by force, but a condition into which the Sabines
would have naturally fallen, had the impulsive chief
exercised a little more patience. The utmost, therefore, that can be said is, that nations recognize a certain condition as proper to the sphere of woman;
while it cannot be shown that even two men acting
in concert with any intelligent design for the future

have ever conspired to reduce her to this condition; while whole nations of men have taken up arms against their plebeian brethren to prolong and extend their dependence, and rivet more firmly the fetters of slavery. The physical force argument, therefore, like all the attempts of the advocates of this reform to account for conditions which they cannot understand, is pitifully superficial.

All the history of the past goes to prove that a system of oppression, contrary to nature, cannot be maintained even under a despotic military government, with the united convictions of those in power all running in favor of suppressing the weak. Does Mr. Mill suppose that any system of slavery would ever have existed on the face of the earth, if so little physical force had been used to institute or maintain it as has been employed against women? Physical and brutal force enough has been used, and is still used against her, but it is the mere aimless outburst of degraded passion, not the concentrated or intelligent effect of man against women, and has as little bearing on this question as the midnight brawls of two drunken revelers on the British constitution. There is not, in the whole history of the race, an instance in which the female side of a nation have taken up arms against the males, nor the males against the females, for the purpose of claiming or maintaining distinct rights; nor is such a condition conceivable so long as the present natural distinctions of sex exist, which make the two really the perfect man. Man and woman, apart or distinct, with separate interests, and selfish struggles to maintain them, have no meaning in nature. This condition is legitimate among men, but between man and woman it does not and cannot exist. If such were the natural relations of the sexes to each other, woman would have struggled to the head of government along with and in opposition to man. She would have taken the initiative in some instances in colonization, discovery, art, or science. To assert that this is as natural to woman as man, and yet allow that she has been prevented by man from its accomplishment, is not the least of Mr. Mill's absurdities. The slave lives his life of freedom amid his chains, and in defiance of all the power of law, as certainly as if he roamed his African plains or Thracian wilds; and it is only because he lives this inner life of freedom that the actual condition is possible, nay, an absolute certainty, in face of all the concentrated efforts of wealth and power. Can it be shown that woman ever has lived, or does now live, this inner life apart from man,—that she desires to withdraw from his society and establish a separate community, over which he shall have no control, to which he shall not even have access,—that she longs to sever the chain which has so long bound her to an alleged condition of slavery? If her conduct is to be taken as an index of her thoughts, the answer to this

is one universal and emphatic "No! No! for our interests are one. We cannot place ourselves in opposition and competition with men, we can only go along
with them; and they must direct." Every true man
wishes to see at least one happy woman. The
highest end of all government and all religion is to
make such men,—to do away with the physical force,
which they exert against women and against one
another, not from a desire to enslave women, but
because they are brutalized, and cannot live among
themselves, nor with their wives, as they ought.
These are the facts in this controversy, and the whole
yea and nay of this alleged system of slavery which,
as it is asserted, has prevented woman from attaining
and occupying the same positions as man in governments, in literature, in science and art.

In face of these incontrovertible truths, what weight
can be attached to a few barren examples selected
from the ranks of hereditary monarchs, where the
conditions are imposed, not attained, and the whole
life so entirely artificial, that little is manifested to the
world of the natural disposition, except where the ruler
is absolute, and even then the force of custom disguises
the natural propensities almost as much as the limitations of actual laws? The tendency of Mr. Mill's reform is to create an artificial state of excitability, which
shall attach an unnatural and pernicious importance
to public positions and offices of trust,—which shall

lead the women of England, like the apostle of this reform, to place their heaven in the House of Commons, and their hell in the routine of domestic duties. Perhaps, however, under the new régime maternity and domestic duties shall have passed away, and additions shall be made to the population as required, on some scientific principle similar to that under which the *acarus* made its *début* some years ago; when from some great national establishment annual shoals of male and female soldiers, rulers and statesmen, shall come forth as required, from beds of artificial spawn deposited by some monster queen-bee, animated by a galvanic battery. If Mr. Mill cannot bring into use some labor-saving system of this kind, it is evident something must go wrong. There is none too much attention paid to the domestic department of human affairs now. The great cry both in England and America is, that the education and bringing up of children, and the management of the household, are left too much to others,—that the mother's influence and the mother's care are passing from among men. "The girl and woman of the period" are too much a reality. How is Mr. Mill to manage this matter when the tendency to an evil already too common shall be greatly increased,—when the mother, with an infant six weeks or six days old, is called away on important parliamentary business? Every one knows

13

the value of a single vote in an important party question. It is true Mr. Mill tells us that when women are
found fitted for those high functions other help should
be procured to manage these humbler details. How
does he know but that his best *statesmen* are among the
Hagars whom he thus condemns to menial drudgery?
But surely, under this enlightened reign of Reason
and Justice, if any woman should be guilty of the
weakness or folly of encumbering herself with a rising
progeny, it would be unfair to endanger the prospects
of another by binding *her* down to servitude, even for
a limited time. Grandmothers could not be spared
for this duty; for among them would be found the
aged guardians of the state, privy councilors, ladies
privy seal, and grooms of the stole! It is, therefore,
evident that if even now the humbler departments of
human affairs are not any too well managed, no
women can be spared for these high functions, unless,
indeed, their place is to be supplied from the ranks of
the "mediocre" men. Perhaps Mr. Mill himself would
be found suitable to take charge of the national population establishment, as he would be able to supply to
order the necessary number of female politicians. As
to the other professions which are, or ought to be,
open to woman, it is presumed Mr. Mill is not advocating her right to take up the profession of a
plowman, blacksmith, or coal-heaver; for no law will

interfere to drive her from the field should she take up "the plowboy's whistle" for "the milkmaid's song," or set up her smithy and put herself in competition with man. Of the higher professions, two only are closed against her,—law and the church. One department of medicine she has properly been allowed to practice for ages. How does it come that in this she has made no progress? Why has she not divided the honors and the spoils with man? No law has prevented her from making some attempt to educate her sisters in this department. Almost all the schools in the British nation have had a private origin. Why has she not established one? All the progress she has made has been due to her benevolence, or the necessity of procuring subsistence. No woman of wealth has devoted her time or means to discoveries or investigations which might lead to the perfecting of what might be regarded as woman's peculiar department in medicine. It is known that schools are now established for the better education of women in this department; but, after all, it is only to acquire knowledge now left ready to hand by the labors of man. As to the general practice of medicine, if the field should be opened to woman, as is now highly probable, it is more from a shrinking to oppose than a conviction that it is the proper sphere of woman; and it is not likely that more than a very limited number will, under any circumstances, engage in a profession which, in all its departments, may be considered as more alien to the nature of woman than embroidery to the nature of man,—although men and women may be found to undertake either. The church and legal profession, therefore, are all that now remain closed against woman. In the church the restrictions are limited; for they exist only in churches having a legal connection with the state, and therefore under civil law. This, then, is the only division in the church to which Mr. Mill's reform could extend. He may, if he choose, convince his countrymen that it would be proper for them to appoint a female Archbishop of Canterbury; but unless he be a presumptuous meddler, anxious to engage in matters for which he has neither the right nor ability, he will not venture to dictate to churches over which the state has no control. Woman's position in the church is recognized by united Christendom. Her power for good could in no possible sphere be more effective than in that in which she now labors. The great desideratum would be, that the duties of this sphere should be more thoroughly discharged, and its importance more fully appreciated. But this is not Mr. Mill's object. All positions are to be open to woman that her pecuniary condition may be improved. No higher idea than this enters into his philosophy. How elevating, then, to the cause of religion, to find woman scheming and lobbying for the vacant livings in the church! It is true that men do this under a kind of mental reservation or conscientious protest,—but, nevertheless, to so great an extent, that church appointments are looked upon more as the reward of devotion to religious sectarianism or political partisanship than of devotion to the cause of Christianity. But how utterly debased must be the philosophy and the philosopher that would set up a general scramble between men and women, for the pecuniary gifts at the disposal of the church, as the legitimate condition of society! The circumstance of good positions and fat livings in the church is, perhaps, a perversion of the whole idea of Christianity; but when these are held up as legitimate plunder for any who have cunning or ability enough to secure them in the struggle and competition, not for the proper discharge, but for emoluments of high social functions, then the cause of religion must certainly be as low as the most absolute utilitarian could desire.

But even as to the pecuniary advantage Mr. Mill is in very great error. If men were all arrayed on one side in selfish opposition to women, as they are among themselves,—often animated not only with the desire of securing wealth for themselves, but with the determination of keeping it from others,—then this reform would have some meaning, and some slight show of

13*

reason to recommend it. But as seventy per cent. of the struggles of men are for their wives and families, or for the maintenance of establishments which *they* perhaps *most fully enjoy*, it certainly would, therefore, tax Mr. Mill's ingenuity to show how much more or less women would secure of the spoils of church or state should his competitive system be introduced.

But in the third chapter of Mr. Mill's essay his most elaborate arguments are put forth, not only to show woman's right to enter the field of competition with man, but her fitness for all professions and positions without distinction. His efforts to show her fitness for the functions of government have already been noticed. For two reasons, his arguments under this head have very little weight, because, in the first place, it cannot much affect the condition of woman if he should satisfactorily prove the fitness of every woman in the nation to become Queen of England, or President of the United States; and, in the second place, the fitness or want of fitness for these positions has very little logical connection with the general question. It is a logical conclusion that perhaps none but Mr. Mill could arrive at, that because woman may be shown fit for these positions, she is therefore fit for every other position, where the conditions of success or failure are totally different. The position of the hereditary sovereign, as already shown, is altogether exceptional, and cannot properly be compared with that of the man or woman who struggles single-handed with surrounding circumstances. ' If the history of single men and women be taken who do not possess any of those exceptional advantages, and where neither of the competitors labors under any of the real or imaginary disadvantages or disabilities imposed by ¯marriage, the evidences are more than sufficient to outweigh the testimony on the opposite side. It is an old discovery, that in the multitude of counselors there is wisdom. It may, therefore, be asserted, without fear of contradiction, that the ruler, male or female, more especially in a barbarous age, who has pliability enough not to set up his or her own single wisdom in opposition to the united wisdom of the age, is likely to promote the best interests of the nation and be regarded as the most successful sovereign. As already observed, this quality of pliability is more characteristic of women than men, and on this alone is based nine-tenths of their superiority as heads of government. Where the power of the sovereign is absolute, this apparent superiority vanishes. Mr. Mill's testimony cannot be taken in favor of the good government of India by females, for the actual facts are against him. Why, if female rulers are so frequent and beneficial, are the governments of India considered inferior to the worst European government? And why are so many advantages expected from the introduction of European systems? Or why even has the government of this country exhibited much more anarchy and confusion than that of China, where similar institutions prevail, except perhaps in what Mr. Mill considers a redeeming feature? The insertion of the note on Hindoo governments tells most fatally against his theory. But Mr. Mill may be further met on his own ground. The terribly artificial conditions under which woman is placed are again put forth as an evidence that her capabilities cannot be known. Must it not, therefore, be true that the more than terribly artificial conditions under which she is placed as head of a government, render it still more difficult to say what would be her capabilities if the influence of these artificial surroundings were eliminated?

But there are other considerations which go to prove that though woman may not be inferior to man, her mentality is of a different order. And here it is not necessary to take exceptional cases, from which, as already observed, it would be just as easy to prove man's fitness and natural capabilities for all the occupations now supposed to belong to the proper sphere of woman. Music is a field in which men and women have enjoyed unrestricted competition from time immemorial, and one in which, if any, it might be thought women ought to have been superior to men, from their finer nervous and mental organization. But yet in this field they have most signally failed. All the higher oratorios and symphonies are the productions of men. Even in the mere instrumental performance, all the great masters are on the male side. In the vocal performance, physiological differences render a comparison impossible, except as to the effect; and here it is generally conceded that woman has the advantage. But even the effects cannot properly be compared, for they are produced by an influence on different parts of the mental constitution. The truth is, that in music, as in everything else, woman is not inferior to man, but different. Again, in the field of painting, no legal disabilities hedge her in or restrict her powers. Yet, though here she has always been untrammeled, nothing of a high order has ever been produced,—indeed, nothing of any account till within the last few years, and even this displays only the ability of a clever copyist. Scarcely a gleam of the imaginative or creative is perceptible. It will not serve to say that the conditions are not equal. Most of the masters have struggled against circumstances more unfavorable than those which surround most women. Even lack of education, and the difficulties of obtaining daily bread, have not been unfrequent. Why have not wives, daughters, or sisters united their labors with their husbands, fathers, or brothers, and equaled or surpassed them in some particular instance? All nature bears testimony that when vitality or energy is suppressed in one direction the manifestations are more luxuriant in another. Yet woman is a direct contradiction and the single exception to this general law. In the period succeeding the Middle Ages, when poetry and song were almost the only literary occupations which afforded pastime or amusement for the more wealthy members of society, and when the education of women differed less from that of men than now, —when, too, they read Greek, Latin, and philosophy, if they read at all, and engaged in the same studies as men,—all the great masters in epic drama and song belong to the male side. Women have accomplished almost nothing in these higher departments of art. Mr. Mill admits this even more fully than here set forth; and yet he most absurdly concludes that although woman has failed in the field where she has been under no legal disabilities, she would most certainly succeed in those from which she has been excluded. Any reasonable man would have supposed that, her talents being confined to a narrower sphere, she would have outstripped those whose labors are extended over a wider range of subjects; especially if equality, in the sense in which it is held by the advocates of this reform, can be predicated of the sexes. But not only has this failure been in a field where woman has labored under no legal disabili-

ties, but in the very one to which it might be supposed her talents are most naturally adapted. For
one of the great prerequisites to success in these departments of human pursuits, is that impressibility
and active sympathy with external objects, as well as
that rapidity and clearness of thought and expression,
so characteristic of woman. Yet, with all these advantages in her favor, she has most signally failed.
Mr. Mill's attempt to escape this difficulty serves only
to show the extremity to which he is driven, and the
absurdities upon which he is willing to venture to up-
hold a false theory. Speaking of painting, he says:
"Yet, in this line of exertion, they have fallen still
more short than in many others, of the highest eminence attained by men. This short-coming, however,
needs no other explanation than the familiar fact,
more universally true in the fine arts than in anything
else, the vast superiority of professional persons over
amateurs." "Women in the educated classes are
almost universally taught some branch or other of the
fine arts, but not that they may gain their living or
social consequence by it. Women artists are all amateurs;" and so of music. This may be all true, but it
is a most desolating argument to Mr. Mill's theory.
Have not all great painters, poets, and musicians been
amateurs at one stage of their history? How is it
that women have never got beyond this? Hundreds

of well-educated women who have been taught more
or less of this branch of art are often obliged to take
up some life profession:—how is it that they have
never chosen this? Certainly their being amateurs
could be no disadvantage. But the statement as to
men taking up these arts as a life profession, is a good
companion-piece to the other absurdities. For, in the
first place, it is the men who enter upon these branches
as life professions that make the greatest failures.
And, in the second place, it is those who, under the
divine impulse of genius, first rise to the position of
amateurs, who afterwards attain the position of masters. Mr. Mill knows the history of Giotto as a shep-
herd-boy, and of Michael Angelo as an embryo notary,
with an enraged and disappointed father and uncle
using all their efforts to turn him from his love of art
and bind him to the desk. The probability is, that no
thought of a life profession occurred to these from their
cradles to their graves; but, rather, that they were led
on by that devotion to art which is equaled in intensity only by the devotion of a lover to his mistress,
while the passion has generally been more lasting.
This it is which has drawn these away from and above
the ranks of mere amateurs and professional painters
and placed them among the gods. And not these alone,
but three-fourths of all who have distinguished themselves in any department of art or science have done

so in face of poverty, and often starvation in a garret, led on by that absorbing, passionate devotion which always accompanies true genius. Many of those who have achieved the greatest successes as painters, poets, and musicians have done so at the sacrifice of comforts which the commonest day-laborer enjoys. Mankind have starved them, and afterwards built their sepulchres. But the divine afflatus by which they were moved is that which has adorned humanity and civilized the world, and is all that is lacking in those, both men and women, who, with circumstances infinitely more favorable to success on their side, have never yet got beyond the ranks of amateurs and mere professionals. If, therefore, Mr. Mill finds it necessary to admit that woman has failed in so many departments of art in achieving the highest eminence, it is only because the necessary mental conditions are lacking, and not because of external circumstances, which, in this case, are just what he claims for woman as the necessary accompaniments of success in other departments.

Whether Mr. Mill feels the absurdities and trivialities with which he has surrounded himself, will always remain a question with those who note the conscious and self-satisfied air which pervades his essay,—a feature which prevails most abundantly in that portion of it now under consideration. Within a very few sentences

14

of each other, he tells us, "woman has failed because
those who practice the fine arts belong to the educated
classes, and do not follow them that they may gain a
living;" next, they have not succeeded "because few
women have time for them." "This," we are told,
"may seem a paradox." It is certainly a Mill-dox,
that woman should be at one moment in such favorable circumstances as to undertake the practice of art
only as an amateur, and therefore fail, and the next
so pestered with domestic duties as not to be able to
devote sufficient attention to it, and therefore cannot
succeed. Strange that there are in the case of women
no intermediate conditions between these two extremes,
in which they might be obliged to choose a profession!
Mr. Mill is, however, eloquent on those difficulties
which arise from the unavoidable attention to domestic
duties, "even when the family is rich." The considerations are most pertinent to another phase of this
question, which must receive some attention in this
discussion, and, therefore, may be given for the benefit
of the reader. "The time and thoughts of every
woman have to satisfy great previous demands on
them for things practical. There is, first, the superintendence of the family and the domestic expenditure,
which occupies at least one woman in every family,
generally the one of mature years and acquired experience, unless the family is so rich as to admit of

delegating that task to hired agency and submitting to all the waste and malversation inseparable from that mode of conducting it. The superintendence of a household, even when not in other respects laborious, is extremely onerous to the thoughts ;- it requires incessant vigilance, an eye which no detail escapes, and presents questions for consideration and solution, foreseen and unforeseen, at every hour of the day, from which the person responsible can hardly ever shake herself free." "If a woman is of rank," etc., the case is still worse.

Where, and how, under the sun, is Mr. Mill to find time for woman to attend to the multifarious duties that are to open up to her, as politician, professor, lawyer, and preacher, out, in, and in search of, office? How is she to attend to the nine days' madness of an election? How find time to convince her neighbors that John Mill is the wisest man in the realm, and ought to be perpetual member of Parliament? When is she to do all the lobbying, threatening, preaching, and bribing that men find necessary to secure their ends? Will it require less time, or will morality rise to a higher level, if she succeed by bestowing her gracious smiles on the young, and her solemn sentimentalities on the old? Men use every artifice at their disposal; women will require them too. Surely Mr. Mill does not understand the nature of the weapons he has undertaken to use in this discussion. If so, he succeeds most admirably, nevertheless, in placing his client in a most unfavorable position for the success of her cause.

These considerations lead to the advantages claimed for the nation from the admission of woman to a share in the administration of public affairs. " Her intuitive perception, her rapid insight into present facts, her sensibility to the present, the gravitation of her mind to the real and actual, her habitual dealing with things as individuals rather than groups, her greater quickness of apprehension, pre-eminently fit her for practice, and render her a very valuable aid in speculation, as a corrective to man, who often lets his faculties go astray in regions not peopled with real beings, animate or inanimate, even idealized, but with personified shadows, created by the illusions of metaphysics or by the mere entanglement of words " Lost in these mystifications, "hardly anything can be of greater value to a man of theory than carrying on his speculations under the criticism of a really superior woman. There is nothing comparable to it for keeping his thoughts within the limits of real things." With these facts before us, is there any more reasonable conclusion, than that woman should be admitted to the full privileges of man, as adviser, conductor, and director in state affairs?　Mr. Mill must have lacked this valuable corrective in his speculations, otherwise he would not have overlooked the fact which has been patent to the world for thousands of years, viz., that the sole value of an adviser, but more especially in the case of woman, if she is to hold such a position, consists in keeping her mind free from the intrigues, speculations, and prejudices of those to whom she is to become counselor. The very qualities which Mr. Mill arrogates would, under any other circumstances, become most fatal to success. The very absorption of woman's mind in the present, would render her the worst possible adviser in affairs with which she herself had become identified. But, besides, perhaps none but Mr. Mill considers it an essential quality in a counselor, that his or her mind should be of that peculiar type that deals only with the present and practical. It is certainly invaluable in case of great emergency and actual danger. Yet any but the merest tyro in political philosophy must see that the great prerequisite in a state counselor, such as woman is to become under the new régime, is the ability to look beyond the present and balance the consequences which lie in the future, more especially when the counselors are themselves to become absorbed and involved in the affairs in connection with which they are to act as counselors. According to Mr. Mill, the politics of women are not likely to be very different from those of

14*

their husbands, except in one particular. What good
end, then, will it serve, adding fuel to the flame which
is already violent, but narrow and prejudiced enough ?
Mr. Mill seems to be particularly enamored of his argument as to woman's ability as a counselor and corrective of man's extravagances, for he has extended it
over twenty pages of his essay, till in his hands it becomes utterly exhausted by the constant recurrence of
the same idea. Yet it is, of all his arguments, the most
foolishly absurd. No one doubts woman's ability as
an adviser, even in matters connected with the state,
so long as she remains uncontaminated with party
politics ; but the hour this takes place all her valuable
influence is lost. Perhaps we shall never learn how
much the stability of nations depends on keeping one-
half of the human family free from the blind selfishness and periodical madness of party strife, till we
have unchained a power which we cannot again recall
or control. One of the greatest blessings connected with
the existing political condition of the sexes, arises
from the fact that it is possible for man, after the heat,
debates, and struggles of party, to return to the society
of a wife and daughters who know perhaps neither the
name nor the meaning of party politics and politicians.
In this society his intoxication passes away, and he
returns to his right mind. This is the great, unappre-
ciated advantage which arises to woman no less than

to man, from the freedom which she now enjoys from the hand-to-hand struggles daily encountered in the field which she madly seeks to enter.

Another argument put forth by Mr. Mill as a reason why this change should be inaugurated is, "that as woman's condition is now highly artificial,—in England further from a state of nature than among any other modern people,—and as Englishmen act only according to rule, and have no other inclinations, they are peculiarly ill qualified to pass judgment on the original tendency of human nature. An Englishman is ignorant of human nature, and does not know it because he has no opportunity of seeing it." Shades of Avon! Shakspeare's epitaph has some meaning at last. Did the great seer behold this day afar off, when a disciple of the most egotistic and superficial school that has ever risen to the dignity of being noticed among men, tells his countrymen, who hold as their birthright the noblest and most faithful commentary on human nature ever given to the world, that they are more ignorant of human nature and more artificial than the people of any other nation? What is the natural system which this great modern self-exalted demi-god labors to introduce? If any opinion can be formed from the war upon the existing social system, and the silence as to the system for the future, it is the natural system which exists among the tribes of the field and forest, and the hordes of Africa and New Guinea, where all sexual distinction, except in its lowest functions, shall have passed away,—where woman's highest object in life shall be to pander to the vanity of some political paramour and make capital for him, till in a few generations, the necessity even for this shall have passed away; for the downfall of the nation may safely be predicted the day such a system is introduced.

Mr. Mill is certainly the most extraordinary man that has appeared in England since the days of Beau Brummel. What were the horoscopic conjunctions at his birth might have some interest for coming generations; for he is the most consummate egotist and twaddler that has ever undertaken in the name of reason or philosophy to enlighten mankind. Reformers have not scrupled to denounce classes and parties, and evils in morals and government. But Mr. Mill is the first who has ventured to denounce without distinction not only the whole mass of the nation to which he belongs, but the world at large, as being unable to see or comprehend what he himself sees and comprehends so clearly. He is also the first who, on the ground of this ignorance on the part of others, has demanded the acceptance of his reform, natural system, or opinions, because, forsooth, they appear natural, reasonable, and what not to him, though probably most unnatural and unreasonable to all the world beside. Surely Mr.

Mill's credulity is equaled only by his egotism, if he hopes to impress upon Englishmen the propriety of a change by which they are to become as natural as they are now artificial. The cause of his client must have been in a most hopeless condition before he found it necessary to resort to this unfortunate argument; for, if ever convinced of the propriety of this change, it cannot be on the ground that the best wives and mothers in the world are the most artificial, as, under the circumstances, the change might prove a most fatal experiment. If by admitting women to the few professions from which they are now excluded, but more particularly to the exercise of the same political functions and privileges as men, it is meant that society shall attain a more natural condition, it must be evident, to any unprejudiced reader of Mr. Mill's essay, that all this tawdry philosophy about the natural and artificial is the merest twaddle. For, if mankind are to exist at all, it must be under some social condition; but all social conditions imply authority, rule, and law, and law implies restraint, and restraint an artificial condition of society in the sense in which artificial is generally used: The only question is, Which is the system likely to be productive of most good and happiness to the race?

How vague Mr. Mill's ideas of the natural and artificial must be may easily be gathered from the hypothetical conditions under which he supposes the natural might be discovered. "If (says the philosopher) men had ever been found in society without women, or women without men, something might be positively known about the mental and moral differences which may be inherent in each." "We cannot isolate a human being from the circumstances of his condition so as to ascertain, experimentally, what he would have been by nature." "What is now called the nature of woman is an eminently artificial thing." Certainly, if anything whatever is known of the nature of the sexes, it is that they should live together, and not in separate societies,—that the natural condition for either would not be one of isolation. Yet Mr. Mill would isolate man, or have men and women exist in societies by themselves, in order to produce experimentally a natural man and woman! Does any sane man need to be told that these would be conditions eminently artificial, —or, rather, so absurdly unnatural, that the sage experimentalist should soon find his colony of naturals, among whom *he* ought certainly to wear motley, vanish from the earth?

So much, by the way, for Mr. Mill's philosophy of the natural and artificial. But what does it all mean? Why, simply that, since mankind cannot thus experimentally produce a natural man or woman, they, Mr. Mill alone excepted, are totally ignorant of the nature of the sexes, especially woman's, and ought therefore to accept, upon his dictum, any social conditions which he, the seer, chooses to propose, as being more natural than those which now exist. The conditions are obvious enough as to their *naturalness*. But the philosopher who succeeds in surrounding himself with so many absurdities cannot be accepted as infallible authority on the advantages to result from his system.

Having thus examined the arguments by which Mr. Mill endeavors to show the importance and justice of introducing the changes which he advocates, the first definite claim comes up for consideration, viz., "the right to municipal and parliamentary suffrage." No one need be told that, once woman obtains this, every other privilege, good or bad, is within her grasp,—the only limit being in the fertility of her imagination and the number and extent of her desires, arising from whatever cause. Does man fear the consequences of making woman politically his equal? Is he so jealous of his privileges that he cannot bear a rival? Or does he value his own superiority to such a degree that he believes woman intellectually unable to accomplish *his* work? This is the accusation which Mr. Mill chooses to bring against him. Now, it is just possible that other men may be as morally and physically brave as Mr. Mill, and that none fear or care much as to the personal consequences which may—indeed, are likely to—arise; for it is possible that, in the struggle and scramble which may ensue, man will be able to hold his own,—at least, that he will fare no worse than woman herself. The feeling with every honest man is, that he does not want to enter the field of legal and political competition with woman,—that he does not wish to consider her weakness and foibles as legitimate capital to be used against her, as all men now use the failings of political opponents. Nor does he wish to see his wife or daughters enter this arena, to be browbeaten and insulted by the depraved and sensual. But, more than all, he fears to risk the welfare of humanity on a mad experiment. The fruits which this reform may bear during the life of any man now living may be neither here nor there, so far as he is personally concerned; but some men have hopes and interests in the future which they themselves never expect to behold fulfilled, but which are to be accomplished, to a great extent, by woman in the sphere which she has always occupied as the help-meet and equal of man in the work which nature has given her to do, but not as his opponent and rival in the strife and struggles of political factions. This is, no doubt, a very selfish and barbarous idea, and may be characterized as such by Mr. Mill, who is among *"the intellectual élite who are privileged to see into futurity."* But it is not too much if men get credit

for their real sentiments in this matter, and not those
which he chooses to attribute to them.

But with regard to the justice of the claim itself, it
is needless to tell those who have followed the arguments in the first part of this discussion, that this is
one of Mr. Mill's weakest points. The claim because
of equality with man is almost too pitifully puerile to
receive a moment's notice, more especially as coming
from an ex-member of the British House of Parliament. Would Mr. Mill be able to tell on what kind
of equality men enjoy this privilege? Or does he
know what is meant by responsibility to the state?
Has he ever heard of naturalization laws or of the
oath of allegiance? If so, surely the absurdity of
the claim on the ground of intellectual equality is sufficiently evident. It may be that woman is the equal
of man,—that she ought to enjoy this privilege,—that
it is even injustice to her that she does not; but certainly Mr. Mill has failed to make it plain. When
governments extend this privilege to any foreigner
that migrates into a country over which their influence extends, and every man born in such a country,
on the ground that he possesses sufficient intellect to
constitute a medium intelligence, without even a presumptive claim upon his allegiance, then it will be
time enough to listen to the ravings about equality;
for, even if the equality asserted should exist, it has no

15

logical connection with the question at issue, as no
standard of intellectuality is fixed among men as the
basis on which they enjoy this privilege.

But Mr. Mill has also failed to show that any good
can arise from extending the franchise to women.
"The majority of women," he tells us, "are not likely
to differ in political opinion from the majority of men
of the same class, unless the question be one in which
the interests of women are in some way involved."
This is certainly modest and harmless enough. Might
not the nation therefore grant Mr. Mill's client this
very small and harmless privilege, on the honor of her
advocate, who guarantees she will not abuse it? In
the first place, if so little effect shall arise from the
change, what is Mr. Mill's object in demanding it?
And in the second, is it wise to give a power into
the hands of any class of the community which may
be exercised in the overthrow of all existing social institutions? Perhaps these institutions are not worth
guarding,—perhaps no change could possibly make
them worse than they are; but it would be a hazard-
ous experiment to annihilate them, leaving society to
remodel itself on this new basis.

It may be said that this is anticipating consequences which the advocates of this reform never
intended. The intention does not enter into the
question. The natural and logical consequences of

Mr. Mill's doctrines would be to loosen all the bonds of society; and the extension of the franchise to woman is the first and most important step in bringing about this result. For, if she feels disposed to use it, she holds a power which man cannot and will not control. If her political opinions are different from those of man, as is admitted, where she is herself concerned, then she must either be allowed her most ambitious or pernicious desires without opposition, or man must enter the field against her, with the same means and appliances to achieve success as are used against his fellow-man. He must encounter her on the political platform, unsexed and excited, sawing the air in wild gesticulations, attempting to overcome or convince an opponent, and he must use against her the redoubled power of sarcasm which perhaps her physiological condition, past history, or present degraded position places at his command. Does Mr. Mill accept this condition for his wife, his sister, or his daughter? It is the logical sequence of this reform, if woman chooses to enter the political arena with man.

But again, if woman should, in the exercise of this privilege, succeed in carrying measures, where she herself is interested, affecting the present relation of the sexes in the marriage contract, it is evident that man, for his own security, must claim release from the responsibility which this contract now places upon him.

Then, indeed, the marriage compact would become something, if possible, even more intangible than Mr. Mill would have it to be. But, though this is certain to be the ultimate result of this reform, the immediate effects would probably not differ very widely from those which arise from existing conditions, as every married woman, at least, would still find it the wisest and best course to coincide, to a great extent, with the political opinions of her husband, as most men now find it to be the wisest and best course to compromise matters with their wives in case of a difference of opinion. But this would not always be the case; and if not, there cannot be, to any right-thinking man, a more disagreeable, not to say demoralizing, spectacle than to behold a husband and wife, living under the same roof, and united by the strongest ties that bind human beings together, divided by that rancor and strife which always connect themselves with political partisanship. Can any man conceive of a man and his wife setting out on a public polling-day to give their support and influence to different political candidates, without giving rise to conditions very unfavorable to family happiness?

Political differences of opinion, even among men, where the parties have much less right to claim mutual forbearance with each other's opinion, is a cause of most bitter, and often lasting, strife. What would this become between man and wife, by whom this mutual forbearance and deference may justly be claimed from each other, though in the heat of political contests it is never extended to a rival? Has Mr. Mill considered that he would be throwing this apple of discord to the brutalized mass, who, according to his view, "form so large a proportion of the population of every country"? But, more than this, women sell their chastity for gold,—would they scruple to sell their votes for the same consideration? This is not brought as an accusation against them. It is a sad fact, and the weight of the evil rests upon man. In this reform, also, he should only place a power in woman's hands which should afterwards be used for his own selfish ends,—which, indeed, should become the principal part of the stock in trade of the mere demagogue and office-seeker. How elevating, then, to the cause of humanity and national and political morality, to find the aspirants to parliamentary honors in any country speculating on the most successful war-cry to secure the woman-vote at the next election! This is no exaggeration of the consequences of this reform, or human nature has belied itself for the last six thousand years.

Any reasonable man, looking at these results, and the madness which so frequently characterizes the conduct of opposite political parties, must at once

15*

see that even the possibility of these evils finding
their way into the homes of the nation is a result
too horrible to contemplate.   It is little wonder,
with these consequences clinging to this reform,
that Mr. Mill should find abundant need for judicial separations; for it is absolutely certain that,
in this particular, the reform would make the food it
fed on.   But this is not all.   The strife, restless gossip, and excitement which would rise among women
themselves must not be overlooked by the enlightened reformer.   How much of this exists among
men, and how utterly subversive it is of an honest
appreciation of each other's position or principles, is
known to all who have watched the progress of a parliamentary, presidential, or even municipal canvass.
Would it be wise, then, to double the excitement attendant upon these, with so little likelihood of beneficial
results,—and all this even in the ordinary administration of public affairs?

But it is admitted that, in cases where woman's
own interests are concerned, her political opinions
would be different from those of her husband.   How
greatly increased would those evils be under such
circumstances!   And what would be the chances for
family happiness, where a husband and wife should
set out on a political canvass in favor of different
candidates, —for one, because he promised great and

beneficial changes in the condition of women; for the other, because he opposed a reform which the husband might consider injudicious or immoral in its tendency? But as to the legislation which might ensue, only one opinion can exist. For if woman, by extending to her the franchise, is to exercise an influence chiefly where she is personally concerned, it must be against that part of man's legislation by which she considers herself wronged, or for the removal of those restrictions of which she complains, or rather Mr. Mill on her behalf.

In connection with this phase of the question, it may be observed, first, that if, by their own united action, and such assistance as they may obtain from men of Mr. Mill's opinions, women succeed in carrying measures in opposition to the general opinion of the male sex, the result would still be partial legislation, and only the exchange of one evil for another. But it is not true, as Mr. Mill, in his simpering, drawing-room gallantry, asserts, that man legislates for himself, or partially, in the questions at issue between the sexes,—"that his sole object has been to enslave woman, and that he still clings to existing systems for the purpose of keeping her in this condition."

With regard to the general question, it may be most safely asserted that any legislation which, in the married state, recognizes separate interests for man or

woman, is erroneous in principle and subversive of the
highest interests of humanity.   If men were generally
in the habit of legislating for themselves, and dis-
regarding women, or enforcing upon them the consequences of laws to which they themselves are not
amenable, the aspersions which are thrown upon them,
for a single exceptional case, would have some semblance of truth, and some show of reason might attach
to Mr. Mill's accusations.   But it stands an unassailable
fact, that throughout the whole range of criminal law
there is neither male nor female.   In the legal ability of
unmarried females to hold, acquire, or transfer property,
this is also true.   The protection extended to subjects
of the state is also much more favorable to women
than men.   So characteristic is this of the whole range
of law, that, with the exception already noticed, men
may be said to have legislated with the utter abnega-
tion of sexual distinctions.   With regard to this exception in the marriage relation, both law and gospel
regard the parties to the contract as one, and man the
responsible representative, for reasons which Mr. Mill
has not attempted to gainsay.   But this is no anomaly.
Corporate bodies are not responsible as individuals,
but in their corporate capacity.   Man, as a party to
the marriage contract, has made his own position more
unfavorable than in any other compact in which men
as a firm become legally responsible, for he has taken

upon himself the whole responsibility. Mr. Mill perhaps has not considered the various reasons for this phase in legally constituted bodies. But, by the time he makes provision, even for the effective collection of debts, in connection with his loosely constituted partnerships, where each member of the firm must become personally responsible, and hold separate shares in the property, with the right of transferring from one to the other at pleasure, he will probably comprehend the necessity for a legal head to represent the marriage relation. Man, in legislating, has placed himself in this position, with the single exception in his favor that he shall control the united effects. Mr. Mill chooses to put this forth as an evidence of his injustice to woman and a selfish and one-sided legislation whereby he is able to seize the property of his wife, and to which he still clings for this object.

It is not too much to tell Mr. Mill that there is in all this the very essence of that insolence which always accompanies self-conceited arrogance, and which bears its own refutation on the very face of it. For, in the first place, this relic of barbarism, as it is called, took its rise at a time when the whole revenue of the English nation was not equal to what some females now bring into the marriage relation. Will Mr. Mill tell us what could be the object in legislating to secure wealth which did not exist, or, if it did, which

was not held by females? But, again, is it not plain
to the most superficial economist, that man cannot be
held responsible for the whole liabilities of the firm
if woman is to withhold from him the control of the
united resources? If, as is now not unfrequently the
case, she not only spends her own property, but con-
trols the expenditure of the whole income, and has,
besides, legal protection in this, and man only legal
responsibility, mankind may continue to flourish, and
sons and daughters may be born to the race, but it
will not be in the bonds of matrimony.

But further, as the law now is, in case of the sale of
real estate, or the death of the husband, she is legally
entitled to an equitable share of the property. If men
had legislated selfishly in this matter there would have
been some attempt, in cases where woman had neither
brought any wealth into the married state, nor acquired any while in it, made to deprive her of these
advantages. Nothing of this kind has been done
or attempted, even where she may have been an in-
valid during her whole married life, or, perhaps, a bill
of expense, claiming less sympathy. For better or
for worse, is the true spirit of man's legislation in
this respect But this is the department where, it
is maintained, woman's interest is concerned, and
which must be canceled on the statute-book. The evils
arising from such a course have already been made

sufficiently manifest in connection with the doctrine of equality in the married state as propounded by Mr. Mill in his second chapter. But one object of extending the franchise to woman is, that she may be able to secure this very result. For here again her advocate chooses to strengthen his claims by a reiteration of woman's condition, which he characterizes as that of a slave. "For," says he, "that they require the suffrage ought to be obvious to those who coincide in no other of the doctrines for which I contend. Even if every woman were a wife, and every wife ought to be a slave, all the more would these slaves stand in need of legal protection, and we know what legal protection the slaves have when the laws are made by their masters." It is difficult to tell whether Mr. Mill wishes to impose upon mankind by playing upon their sympathies, or whether he has imposed upon himself by a kind of lachrymose sentimentality, very near akin to the stock in trade of a professional mourner. Woman's legal and actual position is no more like that of a slave than her champion's is like that of the Grand Lama.

It is not necessary to repeat the facts and legal differences, in face of which a man of less presumption and self-conceit than Mr. Mill would have been dumb; and were it not that blatant repetitions of slavery, injustice, and oppression meet the reader at every turn, no additional facts should be adduced. It may, however, be observed, without a repetition of the observations made toward the close of the last chapter, that one of the distinguishing marks between woman's condition and that of a slave, under all systems of slavery, is, that no change or improvement in the condition of the master improves the condition of the slave. As a general rule, the ratio of improvement with him is inverted. For the wealth of his master, in most instances, depends on his more complete subjugation. But, on the other hand, the change in the condition of woman has always run parallel with, and in the same direction as, the change in the condition of her husband. His increase of wealth has always added comfort, refinement, and even luxurious ease to her condition; while at the same time she possesses a legal right to an equitable share in the united effects. Again, she is his highest confidant, shares in his hopes and joys, and feels his deepest sorrows. This is nowhere found in connection with slavery, except where the slave is lost in the wife. In this case, men and women without law often become a law unto themselves; and Greek and Circassian slaves, from the days of Sardanapalus downward, have cast off their fetters, become equals, and held sovereignty by the strongest of all laws.

But we are told that, from the "enslaved condition of the wife, she cannot be the full confidant of her husband,—that thorough confidence cannot exist except between those which are legally equal." It is most true that the kind of confidence that often exists between man and man *dare* not be brought into the presence of a wife. But none will deny that all the higher and nobler forms of confidence exist only in a limited degree, except between a man and his wife. It is, perhaps, well for the world that the vile, filthy, and criminal confidence which must go to form a part of the sum total of that perfect confidence which seems to be one of Mr. Mill's tests of equality, does not become the common property of husband and wife, or father and son. The fact that it does not, however, affords the strongest possible proof that the husband does neither regard nor treat his wife as a slave or inferior, but legally, morally, and intellectually as an equal. Anything more than the most superficial insight into human nature would have convinced Mr. Mill that every circle of society has its own kinds and degrees of confidence. The same man will extend very different kinds of confidence to his clergyman, day-laborer, and physician, and yet they are all legally his equals, and may be his life acquaintances. Unlimited confidence, therefore, can only be found among the completely brutalized and vicious, who are ignorant alike of feelings of shame and respect. Legal enactments or conditions do not regulate the extent or kind of confidence which shall exist between individuals. The vilest wretch does not regale the ears of his respectable neighbor with an account of the scenes in which he has participated. Nor does he treat his wife to a history of his illicit amours, unless, indeed, she be as vile as himself. The whole thing, however, affords an excellent commentary on Mr. Mill's doctrine of equality, which seems to render him incapable of comprehending any other equality than that which exists between two pounds of beef cut from the same sirloin. And yet, throughout the whole of nature's domain, this is not the kind of equality or equivalency which exists. Here, a given amount of sunlight and heat is the equivalent of a certain definite result in the vegetable world. Here, totally different elements are the constant equivalents of an unvarying chemical result. A given amount of carbon is the equivalent of an unchanging amount of steam, or two or more given forces are the equivalents of a definite resultant. A given power and weight are equivalents in certain fixed relations. Even in the department of mathematical science this truth is no less apparent. Yet all these, by which the operations in the material universe are carried on, differ among themselves. Equality or equivalency, here, does not mean sameness, but often the very opposite. Yet none can say the one is nobler than the other. Man and woman are nature's equivalents in this sense, though it is not necessary that each should be a block of granite, or subject to the same laws, or enjoy the same privileges, or engage in the same occupations. The true idea is, that the privileges or laws which each enjoys or submits to be equivalents in the same sense in which they themselves are equivalents. Indeed, the more this principle is examined, the more irrational, superficial, and unphilosophical does this attempt to reduce the double side of humanity to sameness become. The constant repetition of the terms slavery, injustice, and oppression, as qualifications either of the treatment or condition of woman, because Mr. Mill cannot find this sameness and can comprehend nothing higher, must therefore be placed in the same category as the petulance of the boy who quarrels with his companions because he cannot grapple with his master.

Having thus examined the various arguments adduced by Mr. Mill in favor of extending the franchise to woman, and the propriety of admitting her to the exercise of all government functions, and an unlimited competition with man, not only in the quieter and less ostentatious professions, but also in those where positions are attained only by stern, uncompromising, and often brazen-faced opposition, it now only remains to

inquire what are likely to be the advantages to woman
herself.   This, to some extent, as well as the general
effects upon society, has already been noticed.   It
may, however, be allowed, as the most favorable view
of this reform, that it contemplates the good of woman
throughout the various grades of society, and not of
any particular class in the community.   This, however, is more than can be shown either by the arguments in its favor, or the results likely to arise from
its operation.   In fact, the strongest evidence is present
in connection with the whole agitation, to prove that
it is only intended for a particular and very limited
class in society.   The opening of government situations to women, to be obtained by competition with
men, could only at the very utmost benefit a few dozen
during one generation.   And these could only be
women of wealth, education, and political influence,
who, pecuniarily, have no need of such situations.   It
is true Mrs. M. might attain to the woolsack, and Mrs.
Somebody-else to the budget, but this will not help the
ignorant millions, over whose heads this reform may
wave as proudly, but idly and uselessly, as their
national banner, without affording them the protection
of a thatched cottage.   It will not serve to tell them
that this reform will open up situations and lucrative
offices for them.   The great trouble is, that these situations cannot be found by their husbands; nothing

but the merest ill-paid drudgery is open to many of them. If it were otherwise, the conditions of the wives would improve with that of their companions. What will the franchise do for these? Only render them the tools of those who will know how to use them, and on whom to bestow lucrative offices. Surely there is enough of this gullible element now in the world, without throwing woman at the feet of any loud-mouthed demagogue who chooses to use her for his selfish purposes. What the reform may do for the few women who may escape this inevitable result and attain to the honors in store for the more fortunate, cannot all be told. One thing is certain, they shall sacrifice their womanhood. The rest must be left to posterity.

16*

CHAPTER IV.

IF the views maintained and arguments advanced in the foregoing pages have any foundation in justice, correct principles, or legitimate deduction, it will be unnecessary to follow **Mr.** Mill through the concluding chapter of his essay; more particularly as in it no new doctrines of any importance are advanced, with the exception of an attempt to show the advantages to family peace and true matrimonial felicity likely to arise from his advocated legal equality. Apart from this, the chief feature is a repetition of previously stated generalities, apparently set forth for the purpose, if possible, of demonstrating more fully the good to be derived from the changes proposed, and still further reconciling his countrymen to his peculiar tenets.

Believing, however, that the true grounds from which the good or evil of the system must arise, have already been sufficiently investigated to enable the reader to form some definite opinion with regard to the question at issue, no further attempt need be made to elaborate the opinions already advanced,—a course which would only serve unnecessarily to prolong a .

discussion even now, perhaps, sufficiently extended. Any additional effort, therefore, that may be made, will be devoted to an attempt to elucidate, if possible, the nature of government, and discover the relation sustained to it by the sexes.

It is admitted that this is placing the question, if not in its most difficult, at least in its most ambitious, aspect; and were it not that it contains the whole *pro* and *con* in this controversy, the task should be left to abler dialecticians. Failure, however, in a sphere where so many have failed, has at least the justification, excuse, or perhaps consolation, of a very formidable array of precedent. This of itself could afford no good ground for entering a field wherein, notwithstanding all that has been done, much still remains in a state of chaos, untouched by the long list of philosophers who range themselves along the decline from the lofty eminence of divine rights to the low plane where revel the promoters and supporters of lawless democracy. Here it is safe to admit that no originality is possible except at great disadvantage. Those who have really touched the true theory of government stand so much opposed to the actual forms under which existing institutions have for ages been establishing themselves, as well as to large and influential divisions of the human family, that they are set aside as impracticable,—which means nothing more than that the interests of certain classes in society would suffer. The diamonds, however, which they have dug from the mine, have, in the long course of human struggles, received much polishing, and once and again the truths which they have taught have become the war-cry under which humanity has wrested from the grasp of tyranny the priceless boon of liberty.

In approaching this question it may be observed that if any *a priori* truth at all exists, which may be accepted as an axiomatic basis whereon all government must rest, it must be *that* so generally assumed in all attempts to investigate the nature of human institutions, viz., that man is a social being, gravitating naturally into the gregarious condition. It is true that this now seems to be doubted, as it is maintained that a natural man or woman can only be produced by complete isolation. Such a theory, however, can have no weight except with its author, as it requires no argument to prove that a natural man can only be produced in a natural condition. If, therefore, isolation be necessary to produce a natural man, isolation is his natural condition; but it is not, for then he could not exist.

But, apart from this absurdity, the truth is so generally received in all attempts to increase the stock of useful knowledge in connection with questions of law or polity, that it lies at the base of all theories, or, more properly, the science of government. But, though this be an unassailable truth, it may most safely be asserted that no abstract unchanging standard of government can be adopted as natural to all ages, climes, stages of civilization, and conditions of the race. Any form of government, to be natural, must have in it the same capabilities of improvement and development as man himself. It is only when the race has arrived at perfection that an absolute standard of government can be set up. This, however, is a condition for which it is unnecessary to legislate; for even climatic influence, in the present physical condition of the globe, will always necessitate habits of life, modes of thought, and conditions of existence very diverse in their nature, with their consequent diversities in forms of government, as well as in its administration. This influence alone, which, so far as man can see, must always exist, forbids any form of government uniform in all its details as applicable to the whole human race. It may further be observed, that the occupations, kinds of enterprise, and consequent legal enactments depend almost solely upon this cause. Even the possibility of living together in large societies is subject to this climatic influence or limitation. A city like London or New York is not conceivable, except as an expensive and absurd experiment, among the Esquimaux of the frigid zone. The details, therefore, of government which are natural and necessary under the former conditions, have no natural adaptability to the latter,—indeed, never can have.

But this is not the only influence which modifies forms of government. If man be a being who is progressing toward a kind of relative perfection, then the government suited to the social condition and phases of civilization now in existence may be very much modified to meet the requirements of the future. In fact, the government of any particular age or people is just an index of the stage of human advancement to which it has attained. If this be true, may it not most reasonably be concluded that because these old - world forms of government pass away, are modified, or lost in the new, such conditions may arise as will render it possible, nay, proper, or even necessary, that the relation of the sexes to the governments of nations be entirely readjusted,—so much so that they may completely change places, or, at the very least, that there shall be neither male nor female, so far as government is concerned, either as regards its privileges or its duties? This is the conclusion arrived at, and the sole foundation on which this reform rests. For it sets every other law of reason, justice, or religion at defiance. But this is just where the fallacy ought to be apparent, were it not that the philosophers who advocate this doctrine seem incapable of looking backward or forward, or getting in any way beyond the narrow circle which bounds their own murky horizon; where they have caught up a few of the rounds and catches sung to the words Liberty, Progression, Equality, and Justice, and chant them in mutual self-glorification. As to the other part of the *modus operandi*, it certainly requires as much stupidity as bravery to set at defiance the whole social experience of six thousand years. But no other method is perhaps possible; for, if the true relation of the sexes to government, under any natural system, can be established, no changes which the constitution of a nation may undergo in being adapted to the onward tendencies of the race, can possibly change the relations of man and woman to government or to one another, unless the sexes are themselves transmutable.

It would seem unnecessary to show by argument that if it be natural for man, under any properly constituted form of government, to exercise authority, lead or direct, protect or subdue, then no change in the mode of exercising these can change the relative position of the sexes, unless, indeed, the fillet and bodkin should become the emblems of authority, rather than the sword and scepter. But even when that stage in the history of the race shall have arrived, when war and aggression, with all the rougher forms of authority and power, shall have passed from the earth, still these inalienable sex types and rights and privileges shall remain, displaying to the world their milder forms of authority and submission, willingness to protect and desire for protection.

The only method of evading this conclusion is that already referred to, viz., asserting that the whole past history of the race has established nothing with regard to the nature of the sexes,—not even that it is a natural condition to associate in families or communities, but rather the reverse. It would seem unnecessary to combat this opinion, were it not that men are often overcome by the boldness or absurdity of a proposition rather than by its reasonableness. Those who are capable of seeing its fallacy, pass it in silent contempt; while others receive it with open-mouthed wonder.

Another fallacy, which has been imposed upon society in the name of philosophy, reason, and reform, is, that because unrestricted competition is the best regulator as regards the labor or productions of the various classes in society, independent of sexual distinctions, it must therefore be adopted between men and women themselves. Now, the most superficial observer must see that the two kinds of competition are of a totally different order, being in one case a competition between the result of labor, but in the other between individuals; what may be true of the one kind of competition, therefore, cannot logically be predicated of the other,—even when the individuals belong to the same sex,—much less when they belong to different sexes. It can affect the conditions of society but little if Rosa Bonheur toils quietly at her easel, to hang in the National Gallery, and plead her merit silently against Landseer, or if Joanna Baillie should solicit patronage in competition with Shakspeare on the shelves of a book-stall, or John Mill lie modestly by the side of Madame Sand, without a single *Hadynic nervous tremor ;* but the conditions are very much altered, both as to their logical connection and social effect, if the individuals instead of their works should be placed in competition with each other, in the open struggle for a vacant seat in Parliament, where, if not just, it is at least common to take advantage of all the failings and follies of an opponent, and where these do not exist, to invent and set them afloat, to be flung in the teeth of woman by the common rabble, as they certainly would be, should she choose to enter this field of competition.

The great incentive to evil in these competitive struggles of society arises from the personal contact of those who engage in them. If men and women were obliged to force their labors in literature and art upon the world by the result of Poll or ballot, as it is proposed they should force themselves, then something of the struggle to be instituted between the sexes might be seen, and some estimate of the result

17

might be formed. Then, indeed, Byron scandals would have a meaning, and a vengeance, and would multiply themselves to the satiety of their promoters. This is the exact condition of society which it is proposed to inaugurate by the advocates of this reform, especially in that phase of it which would render all eligible to the public administration of government independent of sexual distinctions.

These considerations show how far we are yet from grappling with the true merits of this question, and how near the surface both the fallacies and absurdities are to be found.

Returning, therefore, to what may be regarded as *a priori* truth relative to the nature of the sexes, and its connection with the problem under consideration, it may be observed, in the first place, that whatever be the origin of the species, the earliest condition in which history takes account of man may be regarded as a natural one. This will be true whether he be a developed monad or the descendant of a veritable human pair; and the forms of government or institutions under which he existed in the earliest historic ages will be a sufficiently near approach to the natural. But among these the institution most primitive in its character and least liable to objection in this respect must be that under which family relations exist. This, whether it be called marriage, natural

selection, or any other name which religion or philosophy may choose to apply, will exhibit a social
institution having about it enough of the primitive to
afford some glimpses of the natural. For if man be
not an artificial product from beginning to end, or if
the terms natural and artificial have not lost all sig-
nification, then the relations on which his very existence depends must at least be considered natural.
But again, if it be natural for mankind to increase
and populate the earth and subdue it, rather than to
dwindle, diminish, or vanish from its surface like the
dodo, then the institution which best realizes the
former condition must be the most natural. But the
whole history of the race goes to prove that wherever
the family institution and its attendant sexual relations
have been best defined, this kind of prosperity has accompanied the conditions. The family relation, then,
may be regarded as furnishing an example of the
most primitive and natural form of government from
which all other forms must have sprung. If, therefore,
the relation of the sexes to each other in this earliest
social institution can be ascertained, then such a discovery must do much toward settling these relations
under any other institution exhibiting conditions of authority, dependence, aggression, or defense. But no
very great degree of penetration is necessary to ascertain that, if a woman has become so associated with

man as to stand to him in the relation of wife, and
mother to his children and hers, she has at once
assumed a dependent position. Are not the physiological conditions attendant upon maternity and the
care of children the strongest possible evidence of
this being at least the outward actual destiny of
woman? The relations themselves are surely not
artificial; and whether or not, woman accepts them,
and has always been as willing to enter upon them as
man; though that moment, by the very duties these
relations impose, she becomes dependent. It is useless to quarrel with the facts,—they stand unassailed
and unassailable. Woman's condition during the most
important period of her life is that of subjection and
dependence; and if the neutral principle of equality
could be introduced she should be completely at the
mercy of man. The sexual and parental instincts in
man's nature make her, nevertheless, in his eyes and
in her own, his perfect equal and most favored companion, the object of his most tender solicitude and
regard, for whom his greatest sacrifices are unconsciously and naturally made, and his best efforts put
forth. His failures arise just from the neglect of these
relative conditions imposed by the difference of sex;
so that it is only when her subject and dependent condition is forgotten, and she is raised to an absurd
man-type equality, that her woman nature is violated

and her greatest injuries received. Is it therefore more natural or reasonable to suppose that her mental constitution is in exact agreement with these natural conditions and requirements, or that she has and must struggle through existence to the last page of man's social history, a bound·Prometheus?

It is admitted that there is no reasoning with, or convincing the man who chooses to call things names by which they are not recognized among men. If philosophers choose to call sticks or stones, or social conditions, shadows, mental, optical, or moral illusions, no logic is so effective as bringing the shadows in contact with their heads.

This is the method adopted by the advocates of this reform. With the whole testimony of human history against them, they have fallen upon the system of calling the facts unnatural, unjust, degrading to woman, and tyrannical in man. The facts, however, remain, and show man to be the natural provider, protector, and head of the family, the natural promoter and perfecter of every enterprise intended for the common good, the supreme arbiter in cases of doubt or difficulty, and the primal actor on account of whom the conditions of civilization are rendered possible. If, therefore, this earliest form of government presents distinct and well-defined sexual conditions under it, and is capable of developing, indeed has developed,

into the higher forms, the conditions it imposes never
become extinct, but perpetuate themselves under
every possible social institution. This truth becomes
evident when it is remembered that these simpler
forms of government themselves never pass away,
but are all contained within the higher. For, just as
on the slope of a tropical mountain the plants of every
clime and region are found, so the higher forms of
government contain all the lower, and the aggregate
principles on which these lower forms are based grow
into the constitutions of states and empires. Seeing,
then, that this simplest form of government, the
family institution, contains within it the germ of
higher forms, the natural prerogative which his condition forces upon man, no less than the natural dependence which her condition forces upon woman, are
carried forward into these higher forms, more especially as the relations of the sexes under which they
arise are perpetual and unchangeable in their nature,
being maintained by the continuance of the institution under which they must have had their first practical manifestation, if, indeed, they should otherwise
have any tendency to pass away. It will serve no
purpose to say that the man has no natural or moral
right to exercise authority over woman when the very
conditions of existence force this upon him. For they
evidently force upon him providence and protection.

But it would be the most monstrous absurdity to allow that these are both natural and obligatory, and yet deprive him of any natural prerogative in their exercise.

But neither will it remove the difficulty to maintain, as do the advocates of this reform, that, as these primitive forms of government belong to savage and barbarous ages, this patriarchal prerogative, or exercise of authority, must pass away as the race advances toward its higher destiny. It is true, the progress of civilization will render the savage and brutal exercise of power—which, indeed, do not arise from sexual relations, and have nothing to do with them—less frequent, till, in the form of force, dictation, or command, it may vanish from the earth; but so long as it is necessary for nations or families to have over them the real, admitted, or delegated conservators of power, for the purpose of inspiring respect or enforcing authority, man is the natural representative of that power. Since, then, in this simplest form of social institutions, power and authority are the natural prerogatives of man, and that these pass, by natural transitions, into patriarchates, chieftainships, monarchies, and all the higher forms of government, this natural relation of the sexes remaining unchanged, man still carries with him his natural responsibilities and accompanying prerogative. His mental powers are employed to meet the contingencies of new positions, conditions, or unexpected developments, and his physical capabilities are called forth to maintain his dignity and rights in the competitive or aggressive struggle for superiority or existence against his fellow-men or his natural surroundings; and it is only when his efforts, ingenuity, and bravery are exhausted that woman forsakes her own sphere and steps in to his assistance,—but this is at that extremity when it has become with each a true Darwinian struggle for very life. Under other circumstances she maintains her own position of natural dependence and unostentatious power,—the equal and confidant of man, aiding by her counsel and intuitive insight, but leaving to him the administrative power; not making nor overcoming circumstances, but assisting in the difficulties that may arise in connection with them. If, therefore, the whole testimony of human history, legitimate deduction, or the analogy of all the higher departments of animated nature have any value in settling the relation of the sexes to one another, and to the active administration of government, then the foregoing conclusions are inevitable.

But how, it may be asked, do these conclusions affect the conditions of woman under the higher forms of limited monarchy or republican government? Though the transitions may be easy and natural

enough from a patriarchate to a chieftainship, and
again to an absolute kingship, are not the more popular forms just noticed so different from these, that the
whole relations of society to government are completely changed, so that the conditions or relations
which may be predicated of the one cannot be logically
predicated of the other? This is the stage in all investigations of the problem at which errors are most
likely to enter, and at which the greatest blunders
have been made, even by writers of unquestionable
ability. Mankind, in relation to government, have
scarcely yet discovered their own true position, rights,
or privileges; and much of the attempted government
and legislation of the world has been little more than
hap-hazard experiment,—a yielding to uncontrollable
circumstances, or ill-considered but imperative demand.
Before *these*, divine rights, kingly prerogative, and
every other right and prerogative held on the ground
of mere personal or social distinction, have fallen and
must fall. The only divine right or natural prerogative that exists among men, whereby one individual
is justified in exercising authority over another, is that
which parents possess in reference to their offspring
during their minority. No other divine right pertains
to man or woman, not even this on merely personal
grounds, but on account of the relative positions of
parents and children. In the same way, the authority

which is claimed for man in the family relation does not belong to him on account of any superior mental or physical powers, nor any mere accidental distinction whatever, but because of his sexual nature, which, as already seen, confers, or more properly imposes, on him the exercise of a certain kind of authority over woman; while the peculiarities of her sexual nature confers or imposes upon her the exercise of an equivalent, but different kind of authority over man. Apart from these, there are no other divine or natural rights possessed by one human being over another.

If these conclusions be true, chieftainships, kingships, monarchies, and republics fall to the ground so far as they are established on mere personal prerogative, and nothing but anarchy and confusion is left to the human race. But though there can be no divine or natural right possessed by one human being to exercise authority over another, apart from those arising under the circumstances already stated, yet there is divine law, justice, and order, and men have a right to *exercise* and *to the exercise* of these. The great mistakes hitherto made among men have arisen from a confounding of the human and Divine,—the man administrator and the God-given law,—and wars have been waged against constitutions and governments in the abstract, instead of the foolish caricatures of them instituted and administered by men. Of the Divine law, order, and justice, only the relative forms exist among mankind. All the progressive movements of the race have only been approach toward the absolute, —rising out of human ideas of law, justice, and order. The development of these relative forms have, with a strong admixture of avarice, selfishness, and ambition, grown into human constitutions and theories of government, modified also, as already noticed, by the natural conditions and limitations under which they had their origin. The true constitutions of nations, therefore, in so far as they are known, have in this way been discovered, not made; for all their highest possibilities exist as an actual fact in the Divine law, and their relative counterpart in the human conscience. It is, therefore, the personification of the nearest approach to this divine and absolute law that becomes the constitution, or rather the ruler of nations. And it is not till mankind shall have discovered that prerogative or authority does not belong to kings or presidents, but to law, and that they are only the delegated administrators, that the science of government shall be placed on a true philosophical basis.

Here, then, is the true answer to all the sophistry so apt to take root on popular institutions, viz., that all government arising from, or being a delegated authority, the authority may be recalled or terminated at pleasure, when the government must cease. But, as already seen, no man or body of men possess this authority to govern from a personal prerogative themselves, and consequently cannot delegate it to others. All that any man or body of men can do is to institute such legislative machinery as will best secure to them the natural right of justice,—in so far as they are able to rise to the true conception of it as contained in the Divine law,—and then delegate the administrative right. But the constitution itself they can neither annul nor recall, so far as it is founded on the unchangeable principles of justice. For, since no man or body of men have invented justice or given it to mankind, even so far as it is embodied in the constitutions of nations, their rights extend only to the administration, not to law itself. This truth will become still more convincing when it is remembered that all that man has done or can do is to discover or invent certain modes of administering or securing justice, more or less effective according to the degree of civilization, kind of education, or purity of religion, and a thousand other changing and modifying influences, themselves varying from age to age, necessitating the invention of new modes, and more extended details and appliances. These belong to man, and these he may change or recall, but law itself is unassailable. Man has not given it, and has not the power to abrogate. If, therefore, the most enlightened nations of the world should go back to the conditions of savage or barbarous existence, it will not be from defect or change in this higher constitution of nations, but because of failure in the administration; for just in so far as man has advanced in civilization and morals will he be able to comprehend the Divine law, order, and justice. His power, in this respect, will always be the exact measure of his development toward true manhood. What are popularly called national constitutions, are, so far as this idea of law and government are concerned, the merest figment, for they are, in themselves, neither law, justice, nor order, but merely a means of appropriating them from the great Divine fountain.

The highest ruler of a nation, therefore, be he king or president, is but a kind of personification of this higher law, through which it acts, while he himself possesses less personal prerogative than the humblest citizen in the realm, and even this little becoming less as the higher forms of civilization arise. The greatest crimes and follies have been perpetrated under the delusion that power and authority were the personal prerogative of kings and rulers; but the day will come, nay, has come, when it matters little to the world if they were both blind and dumb, so far as the exercise of either power or authority held by this tenure is concerned. For the more men advance in civilization, the more will it be seen that all prerogative in rulers

18

arises from the relation in which they stand to the dignity of this Divine law. If, therefore, they condemn or pardon, make war or peace, it is not because as men or women they possess this power, but because, as rulers, they are justice, mercy, authority, and power personified. In this relation to human institutions they are a part of the machinery by which mankind obtain justice and secure social order, since the mental and moral diversities of the race forbid that each individual should attempt to secure these for himself. This delegated power, not to be law but to administer law, may, therefore, logically and justly be recalled, and kings deposed, and rulers changed, and such other means and modes adopted or invented as may be found necessary to secure to mankind as much of the exercise of justice as the changing condition and exigencies of society will render possible, or require. One very important consideration remains in connection with this abstract doctrine of delegated administrative rights, viz., that governments have not been built upon principles arising from a knowledge of these unchangeable relations sustained by mankind to law, and to each other, but rather from a long antagonism of personal rights and assumed personal prerogative. These have, in the course of ages, in many countries neutralized each other, while the original claims remain unchanged, and are still tacitly held and reluctantly acknowledged.

From these long-established but erroneous forms of
power, rulers have, by the mere force of custom, acquired a kind of spurious personal right to exercise
authority which can never rationally belong to a human being as a mere personal right. All the claims,
therefore, arising out of social position or hereditary
distinctions, are of that spurious and parasitical class
which could have first originated only from a false and
illiberal idea of the relations sustained by human
beings to one another. With social problems, therefore,
as they now exist, considerations of expediency and
relative justice have much to do; for, though no
amount of precedent can establish a false principle, or
change that which is morally wrong into what is
morally right, yet, from the imperfect nature of all
human institutions, it may be that no lesser evils cling
to governments having more liberal and auspicious
beginnings ; and that those which have originated
under the most tyrannical and unfavorable conditions
may, from human capabilities of improvement, in the
course of time develop into the most liberal and enlightened.

Having thus examined to some extent the true nature of all human prerogative and authority, so far as
their exercise over others is concerned, especially in
the chief magistrate or head of a government, the
relations of the subjects or citizens of a state demand

some attention. In the most advanced forms of governments the delegated administrative rights vested in the head of a government have not been left unguarded. The constant tendency on the part of man to govern by the assertion of personal prerogative, rather than through his relation to Divine law, by which "kings rule and princes decree justice," has shown the necessity of holding guarantees against the ignorant or willful abuse of power; hence the origin of Magna Charta, Habeas Corpus Acts, Septennial Acts, Houses of Commons, and the extension of the franchise; and yet even these have had their origin in mere necessity rather than in any enlightened views of the science of government.

But, further, as by this delegated right the head of a government possesses, morally, the power to administer law, as it is understood by his legal advisers, embodied in written constitutions, or rendered possible or applicable by the force of custom, so he requires physical power not only to administer justice, but to secure protection to the citizens of the state This physical power, in the course of ages, has taken shape as officers of the civil government, and variously constituted and established military power. But all this placed at the unlimited disposal of rulers, even with recognized delegated rights, has produced results which have led to the discovery and invention of the modes of safety already noticed, and other counteracting influences, ending in the legal recognition of representatives of the people, the control of the finances, and the extension of that simplest legal right, or rather expedient, the franchise. But that, granted as an unlimited and universal or absolute right, would be only the exchange of one evil for another, viz., absolute power for unlimited and lawless democracy. Perhaps experience has not yet decided which is the greater evil; at least, has not established any very decided ground of choice.

Here, then, arises the necessity for further and still further limitations of limitations, out of which have arisen property rights, restrictions with regard to country, birth, naturalization, etc. The true ground, however, for the extension of the franchise arises from the fact, that as physical power is necessary for the just and effective administration of all the functions of government, and that as this power can only be supported by the citizens of the state, at the sacrifice of much personal comfort, liberty, and even life, there arises a mutual obligation between government and people, guaranteeing, on the one hand, justice and protection, on the other, the power and means to secure and administer them.

If the foregoing conclusions are founded in a correct analysis of the nature of government, then some pro-

18*

gress will have been made toward ascertaining the exact relation of the sexes to all legal privileges and the public administration of state affairs.

It will be seen, by a recurrence to the preceding arguments, that these relations, in so far as they have been ascertained, have not arisen out of any intelligent or premeditated design on the part of ruler or ruled, but out of mere necessity, having its origin in the mental, moral, and social constitution of man, modified by the constantly changing phases of external influence. Even the franchise has been wrested only at the sword's-point from the grasp of tyranny, after long ages of the abuse of absolute power; and no other privilege ever obtained or extended to man is more difficult to regulate than this. Though it seems to be necessary, as a guarantee against tyranny and wrong, yet every unprejudiced observer of the workings of modern institutions knows what a power for evil is unchained by placing this privilege in the hands of the masses, both as regards the use which is made of it by those who enjoy it, and the capital which it places at the command of the unprincipled and time-serving politician. Whatever, therefore, may be its value in securing the proper administration of law and justice, it is itself a privilege very liable to abuse, more especially as those to whom it is extended make up the whole element in which the physical power is contained, and may, by united effort, set all law at defiance. This, then, is the great un-chained demon which the administrators of popular governments find it so difficult to control, to which it is proposed to give wider scope, though the wisest and best citizens of the state shrink from all public positions rather than encounter the debasement, or make use of the polluted agencies by which they are attained, and it is only because the experience of the world hitherto seems to prove that it is the most effect-ive instrument that man has yet invented to secure even the relative justice which had for centuries been dispensed rather as a gratuitous morsel thrown to a mendicant or slave, than as the natural right of every human being, that it can be considered a blessing to any people.

A further investigation of the nature and origin of this privilege shows that not only has it grown out of centuries of strife and antagonism between assumed personal prerogative and man's natural right to jus-tice, but it has been secured not for man or woman but for humanity. The arguments usually advanced to show woman's claims to this privilege seem to be founded on the assumption that the franchise is a kind of common fund or right inseparably connected with government, of which man has seized the whole and left nothing for woman, while the truth is, that it has

been forced upon him,—that he has seized it, as a
man seizes any weapon in self-defense, to free himself,
his wife and children, from oppression, and, if he is
still allowed to hold it, he gives very heavy bond for
the privilege.   How fully does the late American war
illustrate this truth, as call after call went forth, and
the best and bravest in the land were drafted into the
ranks, under the perfectly comprehensible legal right
delegated to the head of the government!   This is but
one phase of the heavy responsibility under which
man is placed, receiving in return, under certain conditions and limitations, the privilege of controlling or
strengthening, by a single vote, the power of government, and the very slim chance of rising himself some
day to the exercise of some public function.

This, then, is the privilege gained by long ages of
blood and battle, and still held under heavy bonds and
many limitations, which it is proposed to throw to
woman without the struggle, without the bonds, without the limitations; for the struggle is already past, and
the bonds and limitations cannot be imposed,—a privilege, too, which man has gained for her, not from her,
and which has improved her condition equally with
his own; but, above all, a privilege, even now, very
hard to regulate and control, which she is to use in a
field where man may not, indeed cannot, contend with
her.   In the field of literature, science, or art, the

competition does not involve personal contact or opposition, and the worst feature accompanying failure or success can only be a jealousy or pride which must be concealed from the world. But man cannot meet woman at the polls or on the hustings, and use against her the weapons which usage has now rendered only too common, without sacrificing his manhood. That she should be found there, is an evidence that her sacrifice is already made.

These conclusions, and the considerations which have led to them, afford abundant evidence as to the very different relations in which the sexes stand to this right of franchise. But it may be further observed, that as the conditions which nature has imposed upon the sexes, with respect to their personal relations, do not change under changing forms of government, these conditions fix their relations to all the other functions, privileges, and duties connected with the state. For if, in the family, any well-defined natural conditions can be established limiting the energies or capabilities of woman to certain callings, or out of the family, any moral reasons why she should not engage in others, then, so long as the family institution exists, or moral considerations have any weight, the conditions which they impose remain as permanent as the institutions, moral or physical limitations, under which they arise. But, surely, there

can be no question as to maternity being a function
proper, natural, and peculiar to woman. If so, then
her condition is unavoidably and unchangeably a dependent one during the most important period of her
life, both as regards energy and duration. It is known
that the advocates of this reform attach very little importance to this feature in the history or life of woman,
—that those who consider this alone an almost insuperable obstacle in the way of her engaging in open
and exciting competition and contention with man for
public positions, are met generally with a sneer, as the
most effective and convenient argument. The condition is, however, a natural one, and must always be
accompanied by unquestionable limitations. But it
may be further observed, that any other condition is
an unnatural one. For the unmarried or unfruitful
female is as far from the true dignity of woman, and,
so far as she is individually concerned, as great a monstrosity as would be possible if maternity should
vanish from earth. Unless, therefore, the object be to
create unnatural positions and functions for those
who, to begin with, are themselves unnatural, this reform has no natural adaptability to woman, as woman.
For, as a natural mother, she can no more delegate
the nursing, care, and training of her children to
others than she can their conception. But, to avail
herself of the privileges of this reform, secure its

promised advantages, and discharge its responsibilities, this must be done. Whether is it more important to humanity that woman should continue to discharge these unquestioned natural duties, or that one should occasionally sit in Congress or Parliament, after much labor and sorrow, both to herself and the nine hundred and ninty-nine who fail in the struggle to place themselves in relation to man and government, not by any means shown to be natural, but, so far as any legitimate investigation of the problem can decide, the very reverse? As to the importance to humanity there can be no question. But whatever is important to humanity is as important to woman as to man,—to her ambition as well as happiness. But if, for physiological reasons arising out of the most important feature in the life of woman, she is prohibited from engaging in most, if not all the active duties of government, she is equally prohibited for moral reasons from engaging in others. It is scarcely conceivable that any of her champions would desire to see her sit, either as judge or advocate, in a case of abduction, seduction, abortion, adultery, or divorce, to listen to or ask the questions, or receive the answers, that are necessary under such circumstances to elicit truth, defeat or confuse an adversary; and all this, too, before the unwashed crowd, who gloat with lustful longing on the filth of humanity. Nor could it add to her womanhood should she choose to engage in such departments of the medical profession as have to do only with the disgusting and putrid effects of sensuality. Every city has its list of legalized practitioners who live and flourish upon these abominations. Are the advocates of equalities, and no distinctions, liabilities, or restrictions, mad enough to include these as belonging to the legitimate sphere of woman? If not, where is the line to be drawn? and what about equality? Men instinctively shrink from the bare idea of a wife or daughter having to do with these phases in the affairs of humanity. But every woman is the wife, daughter, or sister of some human being. What man desires the stump politician, the lawyer in the court of *crim. con.*, or the physician who thrives by the treatment of diseases which shall be nameless here, were *his* wife, daughter, or sister? It is probable that the most rabid advocate of equality, and woman's fitness for all the callings in which men engage, would shrink from these and very many more of the logical consequences of their favorite doctrines. The fact that they have allowed so many broad, and ill-guarded, and ill-considered statements to go forth to the world is an evidence how little these consequences have entered into their calculations.

If the causes which have led to this agitation could be fully investigated it would be found, though they are legion, the more prominent ones lie very near the surface. The cause usually assigned, viz., that the progress of the race and the advancement of the age demand equal rights and privileges for man and woman, as well as the removal of any restrictions, real or imaginary, which trammel the energies or limit the usefulness of man or woman, is doubtless very flattering to human vanity, and, like a sugar-coated pill, may be swallowed without even suspecting the ingredients of which it is composed. But it may be fairly questioned whether the men or women of to-day are higher types of man- or womanhood than those of fifty years ago;—whether the old men or youths, the matrons or the maids, possess more true dignity or real greatness than could be found both in Old and New England at the beginning of the present century. This may easily be the case without its affording any evidence of the familiar doctrine, that the human race is degenerating from age to age. Indeed the truth seems to be, in connection with mankind as in every other department of animate and inanimate creation, that the forces are constant,—the moral and intellectual forces being only latent in the savage which are active in the civilized, while these again may become latent in another form in the labors of art, science, literature, and philosophy which a nation may produce. Thus, moral, physical, intel-

lectual, or æsthetic force, may be stored up and exist
in a latent state ages after the nation which produced
it has passed away, and may again pass into the
active condition, just as the art, law, literature, and
philosophy of the Greeks and Romans became the
inspiring influence of modern civilization. The laws
by which these phenomena in the history of humanity
are regulated, and the forces which produce them, are
likely to be as fixed and definite as those in the vegetable world, under which a definite amount of light
and heat becomes latent in the oak or pine, and
may be retained there for ages after vegetative life
has ceased, but which must again pass into the active
condition before it can again pass into the latent state,
under any new relations, whether it be in the printing
of a poem or the forging of an anchor.

The theory of degeneracy in this view, therefore,
rests only on a very unphilosophical basis; for whatever be the ultimate destiny of the race, the history
of mankind hitherto shows that only tribes and
nations advance and degenerate :—that while one has
fulfilled its destiny and acted out its history, and
may be fast sinking into insignificance, another is
just entering upon its career of greatness or glory,
manifesting all the energy, and mental and moral vigor
which the other seems to have lost, thus leaving the
sum total of human knowledge or power, mental or

moral greatness, a constant factor,—varying, it is true, in its outward phases, from the constant mingling and modifying influence of external circumstances, but neither increasing nor diminishing the motive forces possessed by humanity from the beginning.

The phenomena which accompany this constant revolution of force, from the active to the passive state, and *vice versa*, are that certain races and nations, in certain countries, and under certain laws, religions, or forms of government, are capable of a certain definite form of civilization and development. This once attained, the highest destiny of that race or nation has been reached, and just as an individual is incapable of remaining stationary, so a nation in this condition can have nothing before it but decay. This may sometimes advance so slowly as to be almost imperceptible. At other times the decline may be rapid, attended with anarchy and violent struggles, just as the latter are more violent in a strong man dying before his physical energies are exhausted by old age or decay. The views which a nation or people have of themselves, while in this condition of decline, are very similar to the same phenomena in the case of an individual.

Unfounded hope, empty boast, and futile struggles of physical and moral energy against the death-sickness are the most marked characteristics of this historic stage, accompanied too by a loss of the rough but well-defined lines of moral principle and ready self-sacrifice, which now dwindle to a kind of sentimental philosophy, over which the little remaining moral power is exhausted without ever rising to the dignity of action.   This condition in a nation or individual is brought about by causes the most numerous and diverse in character, which it is at any time safe enough to investigate in the case of those who have passed from the stage of action.   But he who should attempt such a course in reference to those of his own time, can scarcely expect to escape the charge of fogyism, — a term of boundless application but no meaning,—and yet it is an oft-expressed opinion among American writers, that European governments are becoming old and falling into decay, and among European writers, even among Americans themselves, that the lawless elements which enter into the composition of the governments on this side of the Atlantic must ultimately work their ruin; and these opinions are not without some foundation.   For while the immense resources of the American Continent have bettered the condition of a large portion of the human race, yet a thousand agencies have arisen whose constantly commingling influences have produced results anything but favorable to mind or morals.   Much of the evil influence against which

American governments have to contend, has arisen from the fact that this continent, the United States especially, has become a city of refuge not only for the worthy, but for the ignorant malcontents and real offenders of every nation. These, from the easy access to state privileges, hold to a very great extent the balance of power between the opposite political parties, and having but little interest in the welfare of the country, or intelligent appreciation of the real merits of diverse political tenets, sell their influence to the party which promises most, or which can most readily descend to pander to their ignorance or their prejudices. In this way they form not only a gullible political element in the nation, but one which very soon learns to live by its wits,—the more so as it presents an almost irresistible temptation to the political aspirant who has no higher principles than ambition or love of gain. But this element has another effect. The opinion of this incongruous mass is not founded on any moral or religious basis whatever. If, in the course of a decade or two, anything like a definite opinion should be evolved by mutual influence and contact, it is of the lowest possible type, formed wholly from without, and taking cognizance only of external forces, without any inherent principle. In this way the faults, follies, and vulgarities of every nation under the sun take root in this liberal soil and are grafted

19*

on the native public opinion, and serve to tone it down
to such a low key, that much of that sterling principle
growing up from within, not built on the surface,
which characterized the men and women of fifty years
ago, has vanished from society. But this is not all.
Even the public amusements partake of the worst
features of all the European nationalities. It is bad
enough when London or Paris support their own immodest frivolities. But it is worse, and the evil is
greatly increased, if New York must support for a
whole winter the Grand Duchess, the Black Crook, the
White Fawn, the Devil's Auction, Humpty Dumpty,
and all the long list of English, French, and German
danseuses and dance-houses, some of which are pat-
ronized seven days in the week. It is not too much
to say that these in a few years make themselves felt
in the political and religious atmosphere, and that the
effect is to make expediency, rather than principle, the
criterion of public morality; for if the sons and daughters of respectable American citizens find it necessary
to patronize these for weeks in succession as proper
and legitimate sources of pastime and amusement,
then it must be that national virtue, modesty, and morality are in the descendent.

It may be very easy, and even very effective, to
meet this with the insinuation, cant, hypocrisy, puritanism, prudery; but there is no better established

truth within the whole range of natural law than
that man or woman cannot seek contact with pollution, or even frivolity, as a means of personal gratifi-
cation and amusement, without being affected by it.
Indeed, it may be regarded as an axiom in morals,
that man should not seek amusement from characters
such as he himself would not wish to become, nor
from the votaries of a profession in which he could
not conscientiously engage, or from which he would
wish to exclude his son, his wife, or his daughter. A
Madame Ristori once in half a century will not re-
deem the low and vulgar herd who thrive on the
vulgarity and brutality of the community.

But again, the almost illimitable resources of the
American continent have created a spirit of enterprise
and restless anxiety in the pursuit of wealth, which
has developed itself into a lawless and unprincipled
gambling propensity, even in the ordinary business
pursuits, anything but favorable to morality or honorable principles. Men without capital, and who have
nothing to lose, labor for months—sometimes for years
—to produce conditions, create opinions or 'tastes, by
which they may be able to swindle the public out of
thousands for which no real value is returned. The
influence and liberty of the press are taken advantage
of for this purpose, so that fortunes are made out of the
circulation of a cunning and well-managed falsehood,

adapted to the credulity with which any proposition is received which ministers to an overexcited propensity. But besides, this becomes so contagious that it permeates every rank and condition of society, so that gambling becomes the legitimate and established order in almost every secular calling, even in things sacred, till men build and embellish churches as they do theaters, and engage popular preachers as they engage popular actors, purely as a speculation to gain influence and make money. The result of all this is anything but favorable to business morality or even common veracity, not to speak of its degrading influence upon religion.

But Americans have another difficulty to encounter in promoting a high state of national morality. There has never been a nation in the world in which it has been so difficult to establish or maintain a high type of national religion. The same heterogeneous elements which go to furnish the public amusements contribute their influence in forming the religious phases of society, and these are so various and dissimilar in their character that any definite religious doctrine having a very extensive influence, is scarcely possible. The religious practice must also fail where religious principles have lost their significance.

In any country where the doctrines of the Reformation have established themselves, the power for good which has been awakened has its unfavorable side.

Religious toleration, with all its blessings, is the door by which a thousand evils enter. For so soon as human conscience becomes the standard of religious opinion, or the test of the correctness or purity of moral convictions, those who have no conscience at all, or one so abnormal in its moral tendencies, or so much under the influence of vicious propensities and so little under that of enlightened reason, that it can only lead to error, have logically the most perfect right to elevate a depraved conscience, or even a vile passion, to the dignity of Divine law. This truth found ample proof and illustration in the insane fanaticism which arose, even before the early reformers had quitted the field of their labors.

No man, therefore, of ordinary discernment need be told, that if Puritanism and Mormonism, Socialism and Shakerism, grow up side by side, in a few generations the result would be, in fact even now is, one from which the distinctive features of each are lost, and a new type produced different from either, displaying— just as certainly as two volumes of water of different temperature, when mingled, produce a mean—religious phases in which, as a general rule, the best features of each are lost sight of. Forms of religion originating in this way have a tendency to degenerate into a mere display of sentiment and passion, from which faith and principle, but, above all, religious intelligence, have departed. All these evils act and react upon each other, till one creates the very soil on which the other can best flourish. For it is only because the higher religious principles are being sacrificed that the madness and folly of the insane idolatry of fashion and the patronage of vicious public amusements is possible. But even the ease with which wealth is accumulated in America increases the evil tendency. In this dangerous moral atmosphere nothing could be more unfavorable than the luxurious ease which wealth confers, and the accompanying tendency to seek amusement and pastime amid evil surroundings. One of the great blessings of labor, apart from its remuneration, arises from the independence and force of character which it confers, enabling its possessor to resist many of the vicious influences under which his more favored, but effeminate, fellow-man most easily falls.

But this evil influence of wealth, and the struggle to acquire it, is further discernible throughout the great mass of American light literature. Any one at all conversant with this department of current literature is aware of this truth. Indeed, it is most amusing to see how many of the heroines are heiresses, who very easily and mysteriously come into immense fortunes, and how many of the heroes are fortune-hunters, into whose hands those fortunes just as easily and mysteriously fall. This, and the very important part which wealth, carriages, mansions, artists, poets, and idlers play in every novel, no other country displays to an equal extent, and it has produced its legitimate result. If no other influence existed, this alone would be sufficient to account for three-fourths of the fortune-hunters and rapacious husbands in America. Certainly if the number of live artists, talented poets, and flourishing young lawyers in America bears any proportion to the number that figure in her literature, a rich harvest from the pen and pencil must be laid up for the delectation of coming ages. The very weak moral which is usually attached to these performances is not sufficient to save this Dick Turpin style of literature from the low level to which it belongs. Even what is called Sunday reading and Sunday literature has, either consciously or unconsciously, both in England and America, fallen into the common course of securing public favor by pandering to public taste, so that the boundaries between the sacred and secular, the human and Divine, have become completely undistinguishable. It is not too much to say that the popular novel, which holds the prominent place on the pages of these religious magazines, with here and there a dash of windy theology, thrown in as Sunday seasoning, or an opiate to the conscience of those who may still have suspicions that all is not right, is the secret of their success. If, therefore, in the face of all these adverse influences, the American government still stands with prospects of a peaceful and prosperous future, it must be that it approaches more nearly than any other to the true theory and practical working of a perfect government; for it is a test that no other government on the face of the earth would have stood so long.   But the difficulties are not yet over.   America is still the refuge for the wronged and wrong-doers of every nation, and her immense territories have yet to be peopled with a strong admixture of this incongruous element and the kind of native product which, under the circumstances, she is able to supply.   The problem of amalgamating the races, religions, and civilizations of the Eastern and Western world has still to be solved on her soil.   The effect which all this has had, and is likely to have, upon the women of America, is easily seen.   Seized with the general restlessness and activity which prevails in a country where so many social elements are still in the condition of being blended into a nationality, which, notwithstanding its many well-defined characteristics, is still in the nascent state, every form of extravagance in the pursuits and ambition of women, as in those of men, finds more complete expression than in any other country.   Another cause which has contributed to this social phenomenon arises from the fact that the education of women in America is perhaps more general than in any other country. This, which must be regarded as a blessing, has, nevertheless, under the peculiar condition of a nation developing with extraordinary rapidity and restless speculation and enterprises, thrown woman into the general current of excitability, and produced more of the man-type ambition than has usually been thought natural or proper to the sex. Whether or not, therefore, woman has in this country greater grievances to redress, or higher positions to attain, than her sisters of other nations, *these*, and not the moral or intellectual, social or religious advancement of the age, *are the true causes* of this agitation. Indeed, so far as any advancement toward any high standard of morality, or the capability of great deeds of self-sacrifice or self-denial, is concerned, it is not likely that the American continent shall ever again witness such men and women as were the fathers and mothers of the Revolution. Their prejudices, it is true, may have been stronger than those of their descendants, but their morality and religion were of a more ingenuous and less complex type.

This, however, has little to do with the question so far as its future is concerned; for though the advancement of the race be the causes said to render this reform necessary, all progress must cease when it is once inaugurated, since the " current moralities and sentimentalities" are dismissed forever from the new formula of human nature, while nothing higher is left for the whole human race than a low, brutal scramble between men and women for fat livings, rich offices, and a jealous and selfish regard for personal interests, aided by the removal of marriage laws and marriage restrictions, the sacred associations of home, filial, fraternal, and sisterly affection, with all sexual distinctions, womanly tenderness, womanly trust, and womanly modesty. This is the programme on which the moralities, sentimentalities, and religion of the future are to take root, and the sole evidence of human progress, human enlightenment and development, on account of which, and to increase which, this reform is demanded. Philosophers who identify themselves with this movement are of that hot-headed and superficial type who live only in the present, gather no lessons from the past, and are incapable of forming any conception as to the result of their own theories in the future, should they ever be honored with a practical experiment. All their reforms rest on vague theories of human nature and ill-digested ideas of government. On these fanciful conditions the whole interests of humanity are risked; while there is no better established fact within the whole range of human knowledge than that a few generations of loose and immodest relations between the sexes, accompanied by its inevitable attendant,—the destruction of family virtue and family morality,—is sufficient to eliminate practically from a nation these and all other virtues. For it is in the family that all the honor, justice, greatness, and goodness which are afterward carried into the councils of state, the battle-field, and every department of human knowledge and human pursuit, take their rise.

The use which is made of the maxim, "To the pure all things are pure," is either very stupid or very dishonest; for to the pure all things are not pure. All company, all sayings, all doings, all professions, all ways and means of acquiring wealth or position, are not pure. Yet it is in this unlimited sense it is put forth by the advocates of this reform, and the popular journalists who support them, in advocating the propriety of the young of both sexes being associated in the public dissecting-room, and the discussion of all the diseases of the victims of misfortune, ignorance, or sensuality which may be brought into the public hospital.

Devotion to science is a plausible but very flimsy covering to throw over the evils which must arise in connection with such a practice. Devotion to science, in ninety-nine cases out of a hundred, means devotion to the remuneration which it will secure. But neither the one nor the other will stifle the language of a stronger passion under circumstances calculated, more

than any other, to awaken it.   The history of all the
empires of antiquity goes to establish the fact that
their decadence began with infidelity to the national
religion, and the relaxation and degradation of social
institutions.   No nation can long resist the influence
of these two evils, and they are necessarily connected
with this reform.   For though its advocates, in their
lucid or perhaps more complaisant moments, descend
so far from their lofty intellectual position as to speak
patronizingly of religion, and of the Bible as a " wonderful old book," and might even be found patting
Deity himself on the back, in their sublime pity and
toleration of every old thing, and old system ; yet,
when under the influence of their system, nothing in
heaven or earth stands in the way of their theories.

The condition of society also to be inaugurated by
the more rabid advocates of this reform, is one in
which *free love* and *socialism* are among the least
evils ; for if there be any one means by which the
disintegration of all social institutions can be brought
more rapidly about than by another, it is the removal
of all sexual distinctions and the well-defined public
opinion by which the intercourse between the sexes
has hitherto been regulated.

But with the degradation of social institutions must
come the destruction of all that virtue which has its
foundation in the family circle, and is built up and

strengthened under home influence. If the people of a country grow up without this influence, it is not the individual only that suffers, but the nation itself is in danger. Among many others, one very patent means of destroying this influence is that which has already been partially noticed, viz., the removal of all sexual distinctions, under the readily-received doctrine that whatever concerns humanity ought to be the common property of the sexes, and should be acquired or investigated in company. A very little attention to the practical working of this doctrine ought to convince its most sanguine advocates that they are trifling with dangerous forces in human nature. It is not too much to suppose, in connection with the medical profession, for example, that many silly, excitable, and even sensual young women may find admittance to the profession, as many young men of this class now do. What is likely to be the moral influence of the dissecting-room under such social circumstances? But further, if it be proper for such to associate in the dissecting-room or hospital for the discussion and investigation of all the departments of the medical profession, it will be proper for them, in this pure devotion to science, to speak of what they have seen and heard to their younger brothers and sisters, and the sons and daughters of their neighbors, around the family hearth, without the weakness of modesty or shame.

20*

What condition of society would this influence alone produce in the course of a few generations? Mr. Mill and his disciples are very anxious to convince their readers that marriage laws are not for the moral alone, but for the low and brutal. It should also be remembered that sexual restrictions are not to be removed for the moral and intelligent only, but for the low and brutal. Indeed, it is more than probable that these, rather than those who recognize higher principles, would take advantage of the change; but more especially in connection with the profession alluded to. It will be no fault of the advocates of this phase of the reform if cyprians of the street, rather than the devotees of science, do not mingle with the sons and daughters of respectable citizens. But even if this should not be the case, any father and mother, true to the higher instincts of their nature, may most sincerely pray that *their* daughter shall not mingle with a class of the most enthusiastic votaries of science in the indiscriminate labors of the dissecting-room.

Having thus examined to some extent the nature of government, the relations sustained to it by man and woman, the unchanging character of those relations, founded on the unmistakable moral, mental, and physical differences connected with sex, as well as the more prominent causes which have led to the demand for such a reform, with its accompanying effects, it now only remains, in conclusion, to notice very briefly a single feature in the concluding chapter of Mr. Mill's essay, viz., the beneficial influence which is claimed for this reform, as it affects the happiness and perfect sympathy of man and wife not only as regards their social tastes, but all pursuits and professions which arise out of the convictions, ambitions, or necessities of life. This, if it were even possible, would be a most questionable advantage from any point of view whatever. The business of a firm is not likely to be best managed when all the partners have exactly the same tastes and talents. This is much more the case in the married relation. Indeed, the family happiness and prosperity depends to an absolute certainty on the husband and wife having many tastes that are totally diverse, but in which each acquiesces, as the necessary conditions of existence. Men, as a general rule, never can have any taste for many of the occupations and duties which arise out of married life. Yet, if the wife should have the same kind of negative sympathy with regard to them, nothing but misery could follow. So it is also with many of the duties in which the husband must engage, and to which his inclinations lead him. Only a negative sympathy can naturally be expected from the wife. In many respects the tastes and active sympathies are as distinct as the sexes, and must ever remain

so, except when perverted by an absurd and pernicious philosophy. What would be the condition of
the great mass of the human family if all the wives in
Pagandom and Christendom should suddenly proclaim
that their tastes led them to the plow, the factory,
the senate or the battle-field, and that these tastes
must be gratified? These are the spheres of men, but
active sympathy and tastes lead to active participa-
tion. It must be rememberd that true social science
does not legislate for those whose *social condition
imposes no duties* upon them, except a mere negative
recognition of the laws of the state in which they
reside. For in these cases it matters little to themselves or the world whether the man or wife, or both,
spend their time parading a picture gallery or climb-
ing a mountain. But these are not the conditions
which are imposed upon the great mass of the human
family, nor can they ever be. The other, viz., the conditions of absolute necessity impose distinct tastes
and distinct duties.

But this is not Mr. Mill's greatest blunder. In
passing, however, the effect of what he calls legal inequality on the education of boys, demands, perhaps,
a moment's notice before examining what is said of
its effect upon women. Any man but one carried
away by an absurd speculation must have known that
if boys domineer over girls, their sisters, or mothers,

Rats

they do so because of their greater force of character and executive impulses; for not one boy in five thousand acts from the knowledge or conviction that he possesses any legal superiority, which, indeed, he does not, since during his minority the boy possesses not a single legal privilege not extended to the girl. The fact that before his majority the boy may enter upon certain occupations and professions, invariably regarded more as a task than a privilege, but which are considered better adapted to men than women, has nothing to do with legal privilege in the sense of superiority; for women have their own set of occupations and even institutions from which men are by common consent excluded; and should woman to-morrow endow or establish a medical school, or any other, she would have a perfect right to exclude man, as man, in establishing similar institutions, has had a perfect right to exclude women, even from principles of justice,—let Mr. Mill interpret the motive as he pleases,—on this ground alone it is unassailable. When woman establishes such institutions, brings them to an important condition of perfection, and investigates all the departments of thought connected with them, and man seeks to force himself into these institutions contrary to her ideas of justice, modesty, or propriety, then he will be in exactly the same position as woman is now with regard to the professions, spheres of industry and enterprise which he has established or perfected. In this case, therefore, law has not instituted, but simply recognized the right which every individual possesses of protecting what he has originated. This is the very worst interpretation that can be given to man's enactments in the matter of exclusion. The boy, therefore, possesses no legal superiority. The attempt, however, to make capital out of such a circumstance, even if it were true, only proves the exceeding shallowness of the author's philosophy. But that it is not true may be easily proved from Mr. Mill's own statements in an early part of his essay. It is only necessary to remind him of the ecstasies he experienced on coming to his majority, " when, for the first time, he experienced this legal superiority or freedom."

Returning, therefore, to the supposed equality of intellectual tastes and habits likely to arise from what are called equal legal privileges, and the desirable conditions of family happiness said to accompany such social phenomena, it may be asked, in the first place, why it is, if legal equality or equal legal privileges produce intellectual equality, that *men* are not intellectually equal and similar in their æsthetic or literary tastes, or political opinions? Clearly one man is as different from another, and intellectually as much his inferior, as any woman can possibly be; and this not in isolated instances, but in cases as numerous and generally diffused as could be found among the opposite sex. But further. Women possess legal equality among themselves. Why are they not intellectually equal, having similarity of tastes and the same objects of ambition? Or why are not all men theologians, philosophers, navigators, soldiers, painters, poets, politicians, Cavaliers, or Roundheads? Surely the veriest clown is capable of seeing that as great diversity of tastes, pursuits, and intellectual attainments exists among men themselves, as could possibly exist between men and women, almost under any conceivable circumstances. Is it not plain if men or women were marrying with beings having the same intellectual diversities as themselves, there would still be as great intellectual differences in the married state as are possible under the existing conditions of society? The whole theory, however, is a most unmistakable proof that Mr. Mill has not yet obtained the faintest idea of the causes of difference between the sexes, nor even between individuals of the same sex. A mythical legal inequality is the very least among the causes which produce these differences; for it does not exist till the mental and moral character is to a very great extent established for life, and even if it did is not thought of by one in ten thousand,

while this moulding of tastes and habits is going
on. It is too much that the public should be so
gulled by Mr. Mill's reputation as a philosopher as
to accept as oracular his reasoning on this particular phase of the question, while it rises so little
above absolute puerility.   Any one at all conversant
with the history of the past must know that at a
time when greater legal inequality existed between
the male portion of the population of the Roman
empire, generals, philosophers, and poets might be
found among plebeians, and every grade of natural
and acquired intelligence, from idiocy upward, among
patricians.

But there is another fallacy connected with this
theory, namely, that uniformity of tastes and sentiments is necessary to domestic happiness, or true
marriage unity.   Variety rather than uniformity is
nature's law.   A man and woman who should be perfectly equal and similar in their intellectual attainments and tastes, should be only as two silver, iron,
or brazen bells, attempting to produce harmony by
wagging their tongues in unison.   Surely, unless the
man and woman had arrived at absolute perfection,
there should be a better chance both for happiness
and development from variety than from similarity
of attainments or tastes.   Perhaps even a Hunter
should not fancy an eternal hash of human bones,

human muscle, and human viscera, morning, noon, and night. Something belonging to a totally different sphere of thought or investigation might be more pleasant and better calculated to develop both man and woman, than listening forever to the echoes of their own thoughts. It is true, a certain degree of intellectual culture and equality is necessary to domestic. happiness. But it is an error to suppose that this means or must be, sameness. He must be a fool or an egotistic neophyte who is pleased by his wife's treating him to a diluted dish of his own philosophy.

The true test of intellectual culture, or intellectual equivalency to any other being, is the ability equally to maintain an intelligent mental equilibrium in any region of thought, and a well-defined intellectual consciousness in connection with any subject of investigation, conversation, or speculation, rather than the mere accumulation of scientific technicalities, or the acquisition of certain mental specialties, either from legal or educational pressure. When this, the true intellectual culture, is present, variety and not similarity of tastes and attainments gives zest and enjoyment to the intercourse of human beings.

The answer of Landseer to his friends who were anxious that he should marry, or at least propose to, Rosa Bonheur, is a most emphatic denial of Mr. Mill's theory. The great artist uttered at least as

21

much philosophy as gallantry, when he assured his advisers "that he could never be willing to live with one who had surpassed him in his own department of art." His being surpassed is but a generous compliment. Perhaps no man in England was more fitted to live with an equal. Yet it is most certain that, in obedience to a higher philosophy than can be found in the pages of Mill, when he escaped from his easel he did not seek the company of the greatest dog lover in England.

THE END.

LIST OF PUBLICATIONS

OF

J. B. LIPPINCOTT & CO.

PHILADELPHIA.

Will be sent by mail, post paid, on receipt of the price.

The Albert N'Yanza. Great Basin of the Nile,

and Explorations of the Nile Sources. By SIR SAMUEL WHITE BAKER, M. A., F. R. G. S., &c. With Maps and numerous Illustrations, from sketches by Mr. Baker. New edition. Crown 8vo. Extra cloth, $3.

"It is one of the most interesting and instructive books of travel ever issued; and this edition, at a reduced price, will bring it within the reach of many who have not before seen it."—*Boston Journal.*

"One of the most fascinating, and certainly not the least important, books of travel published during the century"—*Boston Eve. Transcript.*

The Nile Tributaries of Abyssinia, and the Sword-

Hunters of the Hamran Arabs. By SIR SAMUEL WHITE BAKER, M. A., F. R. G. S., &c. With Maps and numerous Illustrations, from original sketches by the Author. New edition. Crown 8vo. Extra cloth, $2.75.

"We have rarely met with a descriptive work so well conceived and so attractively written as Baker's Abyssinia, and we cor-

dially recommend it to public patronage. . . . It is beautifully illustrated."—*N. O. Times.*

Eight Years' Wandering in Ceylon. By Sir

SAMUEL WHITE BAKER, M. A., F. R. G. S., &c. With Illustrations. 16mo. Extra cloth, $1.50.

"Mr. Baker's description of life in Ceylon, of sport, of the cultivation of the soil, of its birds and beasts and insects and reptiles, of its wild forests and dense jungles, of its palm trees and its betel nuts and intoxicating drugs, will be found very interesting. The book is well written and beautifully printed."—*Balt. Gazette.*

"Notwithstanding the volume abounds with sporting accounts, the natural history of Ceylon is well and carefully described, and the curiosities of the famed island are not neglected. It is a valuable addition to the works on the East Indies."—*Phila. Lutheran Observer.*

The Rifle and the Hound in Ceylon. By Sir

SAMUEL WHITE BAKER, M. A., F. R. G. S., &c. With Illustrations. 16mo. Extra cloth, $1.50.

"Certainly no sporting book we have ever read is more alive with spirit and dashing achievements, and we can guarantee that no one interested in such subjects at all can begin to read without finishing it to the last line, or can lay it down without unbounded admiration for the versatile powers of its hero and author." —*The Round Table.*

Cast Up by the Sea. A Book for Boys from

Eight Years Old to Eighty. By SIR SAMUEL WHITE BAKER, M. A., F. R. G. S., &c, With eleven Illustrations by Huard. 16mo. Cheap edition, cloth, 65 cts. Fine edition, tinted paper, extra cloth, $1.25.

"Since the days when 'Robinson Crusoe' first gave pleasure to the host of readers, young and old, which has ever since been multiplying, we doubt if any book of that class has presented a claim equally strong to take its place right squarely up to it, and alongside. The boys will all run to get it, and old boys, too, will find themselves growing young again in the boyish admiration which it will elicit even from them."—*Charleston Courier.*

"The boy, of whatever age, who takes up this fascinating book, will scarcely lay it down till finis or daylight appears."—*Columbus Journal.*

Bulwer's Novels. Library Edition. Complete in

forty-two volumes. Large type. 12mo. Cloth, $52.50; Library, sheep, $63; half calf, neat, $105; half calf, gilt extra, $115.50. Each novel sold separately, as below, in cloth, at $1.25 per volume.

The Caxtons	2 vols.	Zanoni	2 vols.
My Novel	4 vols.	Pelham	2 vols.
What will He do with It?	3 vols.	The Disowned	2 vols.
Devereux	2 vols.	Paul Clifford	2 vols.
Last Days of Pompeii	2 vols.	Godolphin	1 vol.
Rienzi	2 vols.	Ernest Maltravers	2 vols.
Leila, Calderon	1 vol.	Alice	2 vols.
The Last of the Barons	2 vols.	Night and Morning	2 vols.
Harold	2 vols.	Lucretia	2 vols.
Pilgrims of the Rhine	1 vol.	A Strange Story	2 vols.
Eugene Aram	2 vols.		

"This edition is in every way a desirable one for libraries; the volumes are of convenient size, the type large, the paper of a superior quality, and the binding neat and substantial."—*Philada. Inquirer.*

"Its convenient form makes it desirable for use in traveling, as well as for library purposes. . . . Book-buyers will do well to purchase this edition for their libraries." —*Pittsburg Gazette.*

"Every gentleman who desires to build up a complete library must have this edition of Bulwer."—*Columbus Journal.*

The Old Mam'selle's Secret. After the German

of E. Marlitt, author of "Gold Elsie," "Countess Gisela," &c. By MRS. A. L. WISTER. Sixth edition. 12mo. Cloth, $1.75.

"A more charming story, and one which, having once commenced, it seemed more difficult to leave, we have not met with for many a day."—*The Round Table.*

"Is one of the most intense, concentrated, compact novels of the day. . . . And the work has the minute fidelity of the author of 'The Initials,' the dramatic unity of Reade, and the graphic power of George Elliot."—*Columbus (O.) Journal.*

"Appears to be one of the most interesting stories that we have had from Europe for many a day."—*Boston Traveler.*

Gold Elsie. From the German of E. Marlitt,

author of the "Old Mam'selle's Secret," "Countess Gisela," &c. By MRS. A. L. WISTER. Fifth edition. 12mo. Cloth, $1.75.

"A charming book. It absorbs your attention from the title-page to the end."—*The Home Circle.*

"A charming story charmingly told."—*Baltimore Gazette.*

Countess Gisela. From the German of E. Mur-

litt, author of "The Old Mam'selle's Secret," "Gold Elsie," "Over Yonder," &c. By MRS. A. L. WISTER. Third Edition. 12mo. Cloth, $1.75.

"There is more dramatic power in this than in any of the stories by the same author that we have read."—*N.O. Times.*

"It is a story that arouses the interest of the reader from the outset."—*Pittsburg Gazette.*

"The best work by this author."—*Philada. Telegraph.*

Over Yonder. From the German of E. Marlitt,

author of "Countess Gisela," "Gold Elsie," &c. Third edition. With a full-page Illustration. 8vo. Paper cover, 30 cts.

"'Over Yonder' is a charming novelette. The admirers of 'Old Mam'selle's Secret' will give it a glad reception, while those who are ignorant of the merits of this author will find in it a pleasant introduction to the works of a gifted writer."—*Daily Sentinel.*

Three Thousand Miles through the Rocky Moun-

tains. By A. K. McCLURE. Illustrated. 12mo. Tinted paper. Extra cloth, $2.

"Those wishing to post themselves on the subject of that magnificent and extraordinary Rocky Mountain dominion should read the Colonel's book."—*New York Times.*

"The work makes one of the most satisfactory itineraries that has been given to us from this region, and must be read with both pleasure and profit."—*Philada. North American.*

"We have never seen a book of Western travels which so thoroughly and completely satisfied us as this, nor one written in such agreeable and charming style."—*Bradford Reporter.*

"The letters contain many incidents of Indian life and adventures of travel which impart novel charms to them."—*Chicago Evening Journal.*

"The book is full of useful information.'—*New York Independent.*

"Let him who would have some proper conception of the limitless material richness of the Rocky Mountain region, read this book."—*Charleston (S. C.) Courier.*

Bulwer's Novels. Globe Edition. Complete in

twenty-two volumes. With Frontispiece to each volume. Beautifully printed on fine tinted paper. 16mo. Extra cloth, $33; extra cloth, gilt top, $38.50; half calf, neat, $55; half Turkey, gilt top, $66; half calf, gilt extra, $66. Each novel sold separately, as below, in extra cloth, at $1.50 per volume.

The Caxtons.............1 vol.	Zanoni...................1 vol.
My Novel..............2 vols.	Pelham...................1 vol.
What will He Do with It ?..2 vols.	The Disowned ....1 vol.
Devereux...............1 vol.	Paul Clifford ....1 vol.
Last Days of Pompeii....1 vol.	Ernest Maltravers........1 vol.
Leila, Calderon and Pilgrims.1 v.	Godolphin...............1 vol.
Rienzi ....1 vol.	Alice....................1 vol.
The Last of the Barons..1 vol.	Night and Morning.......1 vol.
Harold................1 vol.	Lucretia.................1 vol.
Eugene Aram..........1 vol.	A Strange Story ....1 vol.

"The Globe edition of Bulwer is very neat and satisfactory—more satisfactory than any other issued in this country."—*Philada. North American.*

"The Globe edition is remarkable for a judicious combination of cheapness, legibility and beauty."—*Charleston Courier.*

"We have repeatedly borne witness to the pre-eminence of the Globe over all other editions, in respect to cheapness, neatness and convenience of size."—*Cincinnati Gazette.*

"The clear-cut type, delicately-tinted paper and tasty binding of this Globe edition of Bulwer's works cannot be awarded too much praise."—*Rural New Yorker.*

"We repeat what we have so often before stated—that the Globe edition is the best ever issued on this side of the Atlantic."—*New Orleans Times.*

"The Globe edition of Bulwer furnishes a model well worthy of imitation."—*Philada. Age.*

"As to execution and price, there is no better edition in the market."—*Chicago Evening Journal.*

"We congratulate this well-known Philadelphia publishing house upon furnishing so complete, so legible, so compact and so beautiful an edition of the writings of this great novelist. The American book-buying and book-reading public will not fail to place this fine edition upon their library shelves. It is the best cheap edition of Bulwer that we have ever seen. It is offered at the low price of $1.50 per volume, at which price the purchaser gets the best part of the bargain."—*Providence Evening Press.*

Reade's Novels. Illustrated Standard Edition of

Charles Reade's Novels. Complete in ten vols. 12mo. With Engraved Frontispiece and Vignette Title to each. Handsomely bound in extra cloth. Price, $15 per set. Extra cloth, gilt top, $17 per set. Sold separately, in extra cloth, as follows:

Hard Cash.............$1.75	The Cloister and the Hearth$1.75
Love me Little Love me	Griffith Gaunt............ 1.50
Long 1.50	Peg Woffington.......... 1.25
Never too Late to Mend.. 1.75	Christie Johnstone....... 1.25
White Lies............. 1.50	The Course of True Love
Foul Play............. 1.50	Never did Run Smooth. 1.25

Tricotrin. The Story of a Waif and Stray. By

OUIDA, author of "Under Two Flags," &c. With Portrait of the Author from an Engraving on Steel. 12mo. Cloth, $2.

"The story is full of vivacity and of thrilling interest."—*Pittsburg Gazette.*
"Tricotrin is a work of absolute power, some truth and deep interest."—*N. Y. Day Book.*

"The book abounds in beautiful sentiments, expressed in a concentrated, compact style which cannot fail to be attractive, and will be read with pleasure in every household."—*San Francisco Times.*

Granville de Vigne; or, Held in Bondage. A

Tale of the Day. By OUIDA, author of "Idalia," "Tricotrin," &c. 12mo. Cloth, $2.

"This is one of the most powerful and spicy works of fiction which the present century, so prolific in light literature, has produced."

Strathmore; or, Wrought by His Own Hand. A

Novel. By OUIDA, author of "Granville de Vigne," &c. 12mo. Cloth, $2.

"It is romance of the intense school, but it is written with more power, fluency and brilliancy than the works of Miss Braddon and Mrs. Wood, while its scenes and characters are taken from high life."—*Boston Transcript.*

Chandos. A Novel. By Ouida, author of "Strath-

more," "Idalia," &c. 12mo. Cloth, $2.

"Those who have read these two last-named brilliant works of fiction (Granville de Vigne and Strathmore) will be sure to read *Chandos*. It is characterized by the same gorgeous coloring of style and some-what exaggerated portraiture of scenes and characters, but it is a story of surpassing power and interest."—*Pittsburg Evening Chronicle.*

Idalia. A Novel. By Ouida, author of "Strath-

more," "Tricotrin," &c. 12mo. Cloth, $2.

"It is a story of love and hatred, of affection and jealousy, of intrigue and devotion. . . . We think this novel will attain a wide popularity, especially among those whose refined taste enables them to appreciate and enjoy what is truly beautiful in literature."—*Albany Evening Journal.*

Under Two Flags. A Story of the Household

and the Desert. By OUIDA, author of "Tricotrin," "Granville de Vigne," &c. 12mo. Cloth, $2.

"No one will be able to resist its fascination who once begins its perusal."—*Philada. Evening Bulletin.*
"This is probably the most popular work of Ouida. It is enough of itself to establish her fame as one of the most eloquent and graphic writers of fiction now living."—*Chicago Journal of Commerce.*

Ouida's Novelettes. First Series, Cecil Castle-

maine's Gage. *Second Series*, Randolph Gordon. *Third Series* Beatrice Boville. Each of these volumes contains a selection of "OUIDA'S" Popular Tales and Stories. 12mo. Cloth, each $1.75.

"The many works already in print by this versatile authoress have established her reputation as a novelist, and these short stories contribute largely to the stock of pleasing narratives and adventures alive to the memory of all who are given to romance and fiction."—*N. Haven Jour.*

The American Beaver and his Works. By Lewis

H. MORGAN, author of "The League of the Iroquois." Handsomely illustrated with twenty-three full-page Lithographs and numerous Wood-Cuts. One vol. 8vo. Tinted paper. Cloth extra, $5.

"The book may be pronounced an expansive and standard work on the American beaver, and a valuable contribution to science."—*N.Y. Herald.*

"The book is an octavo of three hundred and thirty pages, on very thick paper, handsomely bound and abundantly illustrated with maps and diagrams. It is a complete scientific, practical, historical and descriptive treatise on the subject of which it treats, and will all form a standard for those who are seeking knowledge in this department of animal life. . . . By the publication of this book, Messrs. J. B. Lippincott & Co., of Philadelphia, have really done a service to science which we trust will be well rewarded."—*Boston Even. Traveler.*

The Autobiography of Dr. Benjamin Franklin.

The first and only complete edition of Franklin's Memoirs. Printed from the original MS. With Notes and an Introduction. Edited by the HON. JOHN BIGELOW, late Minister of the United States to France. With Portrait from a line Engraving on Steel. Large 12mo. Toned paper. Fine cloth, beveled boards, $2.50.

"The discovery of the original autograph of Benjamin Franklin's characteristic narrative of his own life was one of the fortunate events of Mr. Bigelow's diplomatic career. It has given him the opportunity of producing a volume of rare bibliographical interest, and performing a valuable service to the cause of letters. He has engaged in his task with the enthusiasm of an American scholar, and completed it in a manner highly creditable to his judgment and industry."—*The New York Tribune.*

"Every one who has at heart the honor of the nation, the interests of American literature and the fame of Franklin will thank the author for so requisite a national service, and applaud the manner and method of its fulfillment."—*Boston Even. Transcript.*

The Dervishes. History of the Dervishes; or,

Oriental Spiritualism. By JOHN P. BROWN, Interpreter of the American Legation at Constantinople. With twenty-four Illustrations. One vol. crown 8vo. Tinted paper. Cloth, $3.50.

"In this volume are the fruits of long years of study and investigation, with a great deal of personal observation. It treats, in an exhaustive manner, of the belief and principles of the Dervishes. . . . On the whole, this is a thoroughly original work, which cannot fail to become a book of reference."—*The Philada. Press.*

New America. By Wm. Hepworth Dixon. Fourth

edition. Crown 8vo. With Illustrations. Tinted paper. Extra cloth, $2.75.

"In this graphic volume Mr. Dixon sketches American men and women sharply, vigorously and truthfully, under every aspect."—*Dublin University Magazine.*

Hints for Six Months in Europe. *Being the Pro-*

gramme of a Tour through parts of France, Italy, Austria, Saxony, Prussia, the Tyrol, Switzerland, Holland, Belgium, England and Scotland, in the Summer of 1868. By JOHN H. B. LATROBE. 12mo. Toned paper. Extra cloth, $1.50.

"It has many of the best advantages of a regular guide-book, with the additional excellence of being reliable as to facts and trustworthy as to the opinions it utters."— *New York Christian Advocate.*
"Mr. Latrobe had some capital qualifications for producing a good book about Europe. . . . The result is a highly satisfactory volume, which we commend and recommend to travelers, whether they go abroad or stay at home."— *The Philadelphia Press.*

"Is a genuine treasure-book for every new European traveler. . . . And if this programme should be carefully studied by one about to start on a summer tour in Europe, and be substantially followed by the tourist, he would secure for himself manifold more enjoyment, and save himself from countless disappointments and vexations which he would be sure otherwise to experience." — *Boston Evening Traveler.*

Lippincott's Treasuries of Literary Gems. *Min-*

iature 4to. Choicely printed on the finest toned paper and beautifully bound in extra cloth, gilt and gilt edges. 75 cts. each; as follows:

I. A Treasury of Table Talk. II. Epigrams and Literary Follies. III. A Treasury of Poetic Gems. IV. The Table Talk of Samuel Johnson, LL. D. V. Gleanings from the Comedies of Shakspeare. VI. Beauties of the British Dramatists. The six volumes in neat box, $4.50.

"A charming little series, well edited and printed. More thoroughly readable little books it would be hard to find: there is no padding in them: all is epigram, point, poetry or sound common sense."— *London Publishers' Circular.*

Mizpah. *Friends at Prayer.* *Containing a Prayer* •

or Meditation for each day in the Year. By LAFAYETTE C. LOOMIS. 12mo. Beautifully printed on superfine tinted paper, within red lines. Fine cloth, $2. Extra cloth, gilt edges. $2.50.

This work proposes Morning and Evening Scripture Readings, and an Evening Meditation. The Morning Readings embrace the Psalms twice, and the evening, the New Testament entire, during the year. The Meditations are not expositions of the text, but rather devotional reflections—generally upon the Evening Reading—and intended to follow the Scripture and precede prayer.

The Wife's Messengers: A Novel. *By Mrs. M. B.*

HORTON. 12mo. Tinted paper. Extra cloth, $1.75.

"The writer has produced a capital contribution to the cause of domestic truth, and one which will be read with delight in many a household."—*Ohio Statesman.*
"This story is pervaded by a strong religious feeling. The story is well worth reading on its own merits, and some portions of it are written with a real power that cannot fail to command attention."— *Philada. Evening Telegraph.*

Our Own Birds of the United States. A Familiar

Natural History of the Birds of the United States. By WILLIAM L. BAILY. Revised and Edited by Edward D. Cope, Member of the Academy of Natural Sciences. With numerous Illustrations. 16mo. Toned paper. Extra cloth, $1.50.

"The text is all the more acceptable to the general reader because the birds are called by their popular names, and not by the scientific titles of the cyclopædias, and we know them at once as old friends and companions. We commend this unpretending little book to the public as possessing an interest wider in its range but similar in kind to that which belongs to Gilbert White's Natural History of Selborne."—*N. Y. Even. Post.*

"The whole book is attractive, supplying much pleasantly-conveyed information for young readers, and embodying an ar-

rangement and system that will often make it a helpful work of reference for older naturalists."—*Philada. Even. Bulletin.*

"To the youthful, 'Our Own Birds' is likely to prove a bountiful source of pleasure, and cannot fail to make them thoroughly acquainted with the birds of the United States. As a science there is none more agreeable to study than ornithology. We therefore feel no hesitation in commending this book to the public. It is neatly printed and bound, and is profusely illustrated."—*New York Herald.*

A Few Friends, and How They Amused Them-

selves. A Tale in Nine Chapters, containing descriptions of Twenty Pastimes and Games, and a Fancy-Dress Party. By M. E. DODGE, author of "Hans Brinker," &c. 12mo. Toned paper. Extra cloth, $1.25.

"This convenient little encyclopædia strikes the proper moment most fitly. The evenings have lengthened, and until they again become short parties will be gathered everywhere and social intercourse will be general. But though it is comparatively easy to assemble those who would be amused, the amusement is sometimes replaced by its opposite, and more resembles a religious meeting than the juicy entertainment intended. The 'Few Friends' describes some twenty pastimes, all more

or less intellectual, all provident of mirth. requiring no preparation, and capable of enlisting the largest or passing off with the smallest numbers. The description is conveyed by examples that are themselves 'as good as a play.' The book deserves a wide circulation, as it is the missionary of much social pleasure, and demands no more costly apparatus than ready wit and genial disposition." — *Philada. North American.*

Cameos from English History. By the author of

"The Heir of Redclyffe," &c. With marginal Index. 12mo. Tinted paper. Cloth, $1.25; extra cloth, $1.75.

"History is presented in a very attractive and interesting form for young folks in this work."—*Pittsburg Gazette.*

"An excellent design happily executed."—*N. Y. Times.*

The Diamond Edition of the Poetical Works of

Robert Burns. Edited by REV. R. A. WILLMOTT. New edition. With numerous additions. 18mo. Tinted paper. Fine cloth, $1.

"This small, square, compact volume is printed in clear type, and contains, in three hundred pages, the whole of Burns' poems, with a glossary and index. It is cheap,

elegant and convenient, bringing the works of one of the most popular of British poets within the means of every reader."—*Boston Even. Transcript.*

Agnes Wentworth. A Novel. By E. Foxton,

author of "Herman," and "Sir Pavon and St. Pavon." 12mo. Tinted paper. Extra cloth, $1.50.

"This is a very interesting and well-told story. There is a naturalness in the grouping of the characters, and a clearness of definition, which make the story pleasant and fascinating. Phases of life are also presented in terse and vigorous words. ... It is high-toned and much above the aver-age of most of the novels issuing from the press."—*Pittsburg Gazette.*

"A novel which has the merit of being written in graceful and clear style, while it tells an interesting story."—*The Independent.*

Siena. A Poem. By A. C. Swinburne. [Repub-

lished from *Lippincott's Magazine.*] With Notes. 16mo. Tinted paper. Paper covers, 25 cts.

"Is polished with great care, and is by far the best composition we can recall from Swinburne's pen, in more than one of its effects."—*Philada. North American.*

"One of the most elaborate as well as the most unexceptionable of his productions."—*N. Y. Evening Post.*

Recollections of Persons and Places in the West.

By H. M. BRACKENRIDGE, a native of the West; Traveler, Author Jurist. New edition, enlarged. 12mo. Toned paper. Fine cloth, $2.

"A very pleasant book it is, describing, in an autobiographical form, what was 'The West' of this country half a century ago."—*Philada. Press.*

"The writer of these 'Recollections' was born in 1786, and his book is accordingly full of interesting facts and anecdotes respecting a period of Western history, which, when the rapid growth of the country is considered, may almost be called Pre-Adamite."—*Boston Evening Transcript.*

Infelicia. A Volume of Poems. By Adah Isaacs

MENKEN. 16mo. Toned paper. Neat cloth, $1. Paper cover, 75 cts. With Portrait of Author, and Letter of Mr. Charles Dickens, from a Steel Engraving. Fine cloth, beveled boards, gilt top, $1.50.

"Some of the poems are forcible, others are graceful and tender, but all are pervaded by a spirit of sadness."—*Washington Evening Star.*

"The volume is interesting, as revealing a something that lay beyond the vulgar eyes that took the liberty of license with the living author's form, and it serves to drape the unhappy life with the mantle of a proper human charity. For herein are visible the vague reachings after and reminiscences of higher things." — *Cincinnati Evening Chronicle.*

Dallas Galbraith. A Novel. By Mrs. R. Hard-

ING DAVIS, author of "Waiting for the Verdict," "Margaret Howth," "Life in the Iron Mills," &c. 8vo. Fine cloth, $2.

"One of the best novels ever written for an American magazine."—*Philada. Morning Post.*

"The story is most happily written in all respects."—*The North American.*

"As a specimen of her wonderful intensity and passionate sympathies, this sustained and wholly noble romance is equal or superior to any previous achievement."—*Philada. Evening Bulletin.*

"We therefore seize the opportunity to say that this is a story of unusual power, opening so as to awaken interest and maintaining the interest to the end."—*The National Baptist.*

Beatrice. A Poem. By Hon. Roden Noel.

Square 16mo. Tinted paper. Extra cloth, gilt top, $1.

"It is impossible to read the poem through without being powerfully moved. There are passages in it which for intensity and tenderness, clear and vivid vision, spontaneous and delicate sympathy, may be compared with the best efforts of our best living writers."—*London Spectator.*

"Mr. Noel has a fruitful imagination, and such a thorough command of language as to link the heart and tongue in that union from which only true poesy is born." —*N. O. Times.*

"Mr. Noel has no rival. He sings with fairy-like and subtle power." —*London Athenæum.*

Breaking a Butterfly; or, Blanche Ellerslie's

Ending. A Novel. By the author of "Guy Livingstone," &c. Author's Edition. With Illustrations. 12mo. Extra cloth, $1.50. Paper cover, 50 cts.

"It is a charming story of English life, and marked by the well-known characteristics of the author's style, in which the gorgeous descriptions of manhood are predominant."—*Buffalo Express.*

"It is intensely interesting, full of life and spirit, and throughout is written in the gifted author's most captivating vein."—*Philada. Age.*

"It is a story which every one will find interesting ; and it is written with an easy grace indicative of good taste and large experience."—*Albany Journal.*

The Voice in Singing. From the German of

Emma Seiler. Third edition. 12mo. Tinted paper. Extra cloth, $1.50.

"We would earnestly advise all interested in any way in the vocal organs to read and thoroughly digest this remarkable work."—*Boston Musical Times.*

"It is meeting with the favor of all our authorities, and is a very valuable work. To any one engaged in teaching cultivation of the voice, or making singing a study, it will prove an efficient assistant."—*Loomis' Musical Journal.*

"This remarkable book is of special interest to teachers and scholars of vocal music. It is, however, of value to that much larger number of persons who love music for its own sake. Here, almost for the first time in English, and certainly for the first time in an American book, we have a satisfactory explanation of the physiology and æsthetics of the art divine."—*Philada. North American.*

Abraham Page, Esq. Life and Opinions of

Abraham Page, Esq. 12mo. Tinted paper. Fine cloth, $1.50.

"It is really refreshing, in these days of sensational stuff, to fall upon a book like this, written with the easy, well-bred air of a gentleman, and the grace and culture of a scholar."—*Baltimore Leader.*

What I Know about Ben Eccles. A Novel. By

ABRAHAM PAGE, author of "The Life and Opinions of Abraham Page, Esq." 12mo. Cloth, $1.50.

"Quite a pathetic story, which, without being at all of the kind denominated *sen-* *sational,* will enchain the attention to the very close."—*Pittsburg Ev. Journal.*